WRATH AND WING

ENA OF ILBREA, THE BEGINNING

MEGAN O'RUSSELL

Ink Worlds Press

Visit our website at www.MeganORussell.com

Wrath and Wing

Cover Art by Sleepy Fox Studio (https://www.sleepyfoxstudio.net/)

Editing by Christopher Russell

Interior Design by Christopher Russell

Printed in the United States of America

WRATH AND WING

There is a world outside the village of Harane. Beyond the towering mountains to the east and the open skies to the west. Beyond Ilbrea and the seven Guilds that rule our country with a golden fist.

There is an ocean where free men sail to lands beyond my imagination. There are countries ruled by good and just leaders. There are places where magic is more than a thing to be feared.

But I do not live in any of those places. I live in Harane.

I was born in Harane, my parents died in Harane. And as I stood in the field, blood surrounding my boots, it felt as though the outside world might be a lie.

There was nothing in existence but pain and death, and there was no chance of surviving if a person was fool enough to hold on to the dream that something more could be found.

"You've got to save him." Handor knelt beside his son, pushing the boy's hair away from his face as though it might somehow spare his life. "Jesep. Hold on, Jesep. Ena is here."

He said my name like there was something I could do.

"Please, Ena." Tears streamed down Handor's face.

I'd hardly ever seen the man smile, let alone cry.

The wound was too big for me to mend. The fool Jesep had let his axe strike his leg instead of the wood he'd been cutting. By the time Karin had dragged me to Handor's home, the axe had been pulled from Jesep's thigh, and mud had somehow smeared into the wound.

"Give me your shirt." I knelt by Jesep's leg.

Handor struggled out of the sweat-soaked fabric.

I tied the shirt just above the gash, but there was already too much blood on the ground.

"Hold on, boy," Handor said.

"Ena, is there anything I can do?" Karin asked, her back still turned to the whole bloody scene.

I wanted to scream that there was nothing any of us could do.

Even if a Guilded healer raced up on horseback, there was nothing but magic or the gods that could save the boy's life.

But I wasn't strong enough to say that to his father.

"Run and grab the brown jug from under the table at Lily's," I said.

Karin sprinted away. By the time she got back, Jesep would be dead, but Karin didn't need to listen to the boy's final breaths.

I dragged the cutting block over and flipped it on its side.

"Hold his head up." I lifted Jesep's legs onto the block as his father cradled his head.

Jesep gave an awful gasp. The blood flowing from the wound had slowed. It had nothing to do with the cloth I'd tied above it.

"Speak to him." I knelt, feeling the warmth of Jesep's blood seep through the knees of my skirt.

"You're going to be just fine, boy," Handor said. "Ena will get you stitched up. You won't be able to work for a bit. You'll miss the spring planting. You've always hated the planting, and you'll get to rest this year."

I ripped the slash in Jesep's pants wider so I could get a better look at the wound. The axe had cut well beyond stitches' ability to remedy.

"How does it look?" Handor asked. "Do you need help?"

"Just keep talking to him." I couldn't bring myself to press on the wound. I wouldn't cause Jesep any more agony in his last moments, even to comfort his father.

"Just hold on, son. I'm right here, so hold on."

Jesep took a shuddering breath, and fled from his pain.

"No!" Handor's cry sent the ravens scattering from their perches in the trees. "Wake up, son. I am your father, and I am telling you to wake up."

"I'm sorry." I didn't reach out to comfort him—there was too much of his son's blood covering my hands.

Handor's cries beckoned the rest of the village like a siren's song. The few who had been lingering by the corner of the house left the safety of the shadows, and more appeared every moment, coming to see what new grief had stricken Harane.

"We should get him into the house." Shilv ran a hand through the fluff of his graying hair. "Come on, Handor, let's get the boy inside."

Other men from the village came forward to help carry Jesep.

I faded to the back of the group.

Next would come finding money to pay for the burial papers, deciding who would dig the grave, and settling the family into mourning. I could help with none of those things.

I kept my hands in front of me as I made my way back to Lily's house. My skirt was already covered in mud and blood, but wiping my hands on the fabric seemed like it would somehow make everything worse.

Karin raced toward me, brown jug in hand. Her steps faltered as she stared at the blood on my clothes. She nodded and kept heading for Handor's house, her steps slower now that there was no reason to run.

I hoped the jug could be of some comfort. Lily had brewed the liquor to clean wounds, but Handor would be far beyond caring how foul his drink tasted.

The giant tree waited in front of Lily's house when I arrived home. The barren branches looked the same as they had when I'd sprinted away. It seemed impossible that the shadows the tree cast across the road hadn't changed. Death had come so quickly, the afternoon sun had barely shifted.

I wanted to climb up into the safety of the tree's limbs. To peer at the world from high above and see if Handor's pain was somehow justified when viewed by the stars.

Better yet, I could run for the safety of the mountains, where no one would dare to follow me, and pretend Jesep was still alive.

But the proof of his death was sticky on my hands, and I'd waded through enough blood and grief to know I couldn't hide from the pointless reality of Jesep's fate.

I shouldered open the gate to the back garden, hoping Lily had returned from helping deliver Bida's baby.

The garden was empty. I stood at the door to the house for a while, staring at the latch. There was no way to get inside without touching anything and no way to wash Jesep's blood off my hands without getting in to the sink.

I pressed my forehead against the sun-warmed wood of the door.

"Ena?"

I jumped at the sound of Cal's voice, knocking my elbow into the door as I spun around.

Cal's eyes went wide as he stared at me, but his voice was level as he spoke. "I just came from Handor's. I heard you'd been there."

"Lily's with Bida," I said. "Poor woman's been in labor far too long."

"Have they sent to Nantic for the Guilded healer?" Cal opened the door for me.

The scent of dried flowers and herbs cut through the metallic stench of blood.

"Someone rode out this morning," I said. "If they're lucky, the Guilded healer might arrive during the night."

"I'm sure Bida will be fine." Cal worked the handle on the sink pump. "How many babies has Lily delivered?"

"Half the village." I scrubbed my hands, digging my nails into the thick brick of soap to purge the red from beneath them. "That doesn't mean Bida or her baby will survive."

"Ena—"

"Lily isn't a proper healer. I'm nowhere near a proper healer."

"You two are the best Harane has. When people are ill, they hardly ever have the time or coin to go the thirty miles to Nantic for the Guilds' chivving healer."

"So it becomes my happy duty to watch people die? If the Guilds found out Lily was helping Bida, or that I had been fool enough to think I could help Jesep, she and I would both be hanged. And for what? So I can end up with blood all over my hands and Jesep can still end up dead?"

"Would anyone have been able to help Jesep?" Cal picked up a cloth and took my hands in his, tenderly drying my fingers as they trembled. "Ena, would they?"

"I don't think so." The thought sent pain to my throat. "The wound went clean to the bone, and he'd gotten mud in it. Even if someone had been able to stop the bleeding, he would have died of infection."

"Then you did everything anyone could have asked of you."

"A back alley healer who watches people die. This is the life I lead. I'm supposed to be training as an ink maker, not a half-mad butcher with some herbs for a fever."

Cal folded the cloth and tucked it by the sink.

I thought he'd given up on speaking to me.

When he turned back around, a foreign glint filled his eyes. "You are strong and incredible. You and Lily run around helping people because there's not another soul in Harane brave enough to try." He tucked my hair behind my ears. "You do it because we need you, Ena."

He leaned in and kissed me gently, like I was something precious that might break. He tasted familiar, like warm honey in the winter. He rested his forehead against mine.

I wanted to lean into him, to accept his comfort, but Jesep's blood still covered my skirt.

"I should change."

He pressed his lips to my forehead. "I'll make you some tea."

I cut around the big table that took up most of the main room. I'd been working when Karin had run screaming into the house. I'd spilled the ink I'd been making as I chased after her.

The blood and mud on my skirt I might be able to clean. The deep purple ink spot on the table would be permanent.

I stopped in front of the ladder to the loft where I slept,

debating between touching my skirt to keep it from dragging on my way up or keeping my hands clean and letting the bloody fabric leave a mess on the rungs.

My fingers fumbled as I undid the buttons that held my skirt up. The rush of energy from racing to help had started to wear off, and my limbs felt as though they'd been packed with stones.

"Ena!" A clang came from near the stove as I dropped my skirt to the ground, leaving only my shift covering down to my knees.

"What?" I turned to Cal, whose eyes had gone even wider than when I'd been smeared with blood. "Don't look if you're going to blush about it."

I climbed my ladder.

"If it had been another boy from the village instead of me, would you still have taken your skirt off?" Cal called up.

"I suppose that depends."

The sounds of movement from below stopped.

"On what?"

"If they'd offered to make me tea."

I opened the trunk that held the few things I owned, biting back my laughter as Cal muttered below.

"Are you all right down there, Cal?" I fastened a deep blue skirt around my waist.

"Just coming up with ways to keep every other boy with tea away from you."

I liked the way Cal made me laugh. From covered in blood to joking about flirting with other boys. Cal made things easy like that.

He pressed a cup of tea into my hands as soon as I got down the ladder and leaned against the table as I went back to my inking work. I could almost pretend life was happy as I ground roots into paste and made pretty inks to be sold to faraway cities.

Cal's blond hair and bright blue eyes were like something out of a story where the girl lives happily ever after. But even his smile couldn't change the fact that healing salves hid under the floorboards.

Soon, someone else would want my help, and I didn't know if I would be able to do anything but watch them die. Unless the Guilds found me out first. Then I would be dead before anyone had need of me.

Sleep didn't come easily that night. Cal had left when the sun began to set and he knew his parents would be looking for him.

I lay alone in my loft, staring through the darkness to the wooden beams above me, trying to convince myself I should sleep. But closing my eyes would allow dreams, and I'd had enough horror during the day. I didn't need to face any more in my own mind.

Sleep had finally swallowed me when the door swung open. I gasped and sat up, groping around my cot to find something to defend myself with.

"Go back to sleep, girl." Lily stood in the doorway, the faint moonlight glistening off her silver hair.

"Did the healer come from Nantic?" I pressed my hand to my chest, willing my heart to slow.

"Yes." Lily closed the door, shutting out the light.

I squinted to see her shadow as she knelt, tucking her basket of illegal remedies back into the gap beneath the floorboards.

"Do you think Bida will be all right?" I asked.

"It's in the hands of the Guilds now." Lily kicked off her boots and disappeared behind the curtain that separated her sleeping space from the work room.

Part of me wondered if I should be as good as Cal. Crawl down my ladder, put the kettle on the stove, and force Lily to drink a cup of tea whether she liked it or not.

But the rest of me was too angry.

Furious at the Guilds for forcing Lily to sneak away without knowing if Bida or her baby would survive. For making the woman who had helped so many of us creep through the dark like a criminal.

I was angry with Lily, too. For getting herself into such a position in the first place. For teaching me the bare bit of healing I knew so I would be a terrible chivving person to refuse to help someone in need, even if the last thing I wanted was another's life in my hands.

My blankets didn't bring any comfort as I lay back down in my bed.

The whole day would repeat again. The people needing help would be different, but the outcome would be the same. Lily and I would risk our necks, and Harane would lose another citizen. The horrible cycle would repeat until it was my turn to be buried.

I rolled over, clutching the blankets to my chin, pressing down my urge to spring from bed, run into the darkness, and never come back.

I wished I believed in wishes. That I could look up to the stars glimmering above the eastern mountains and wish for a life away from Harane.

When I was very little, my brother Emmet had told me such wishes could come true. We'd sit outside our parents' home, and I would wish for a horse that could run faster than the wind, or a tree to climb that grew higher than the mountains, or a dress made of every color that had ever existed. My brother would laugh and tell me to keep wishing so the stars could hear my plea.

But that was when I believed in such nonsense. The child I

was had parents and hope. Lying in the loft, all I had was Lily and the sure knowledge that wishes did not come true, despite the comforting lies my brother had told me.

The horrible ache of missing Emmet clenched my gut. I wanted to see my brother, to tell him everything that had happened and let him feed me a beautiful lie I could believe for one shining moment. But he was all the way in Nantic, working in the blacksmith's shop. Seeing him would mean sneaking away from Lily, traveling on the mountain road by myself, and leaving Harane.

The missing turned into an itching that crept down to my legs, begging me to leap out of bed and run. I closed my eyes, waiting for sleep to take me or sense to return.

When the first rays of sun peered through the windows, the itching still hadn't stopped. So, I pulled my heavy shawl from my trunk, took my bag from its place by the door, and left a note on the worktable for Lily.

The weight of what I'd done didn't hit me as I crept out of the garden. Lily hadn't slept for more than a day, and being quiet as I left was simply my being kind. And walking down the road through the center of the village wasn't odd at all. Perhaps I was out a bit earlier than usual, but there was nothing wrong with that.

I reached the northern edge of the village and the packed dirt square where the people of Harane gathered for every occasion that required a crowd. It wasn't until I stepped beyond the square and passed the boundary of the village that I truly realized I was leaving. I'd made my decision.

I was going to walk to Nantic and find my brother.

And I would never return to Harane.

The village of Harane is on the mountain road, which runs north to south through the country of Ilbrea. I don't know how old the road is, or who placed it close enough to the edge of the eastern mountain range that travelers are terrified of ghosts dragging them into the forest. I don't even know when the stories of shadows in the woods began.

I do know I've seen grown men tremble at the mere thought of venturing into the forest.

I also know the mountain road is the only reason for Harane to exist. The village where I'd spent my whole life was nothing more than a stopping place for travelers and traders as they made their way someplace else. The closest places being Hareford twenty-nine miles south of Harane, and Nantic thirty miles north of Harane. A solid day's travel between my home and a chance at anything different.

I tried not to think of the distance as I walked north on the mountain road. I'd made the journey a few times before my parents died. Once Lily had taken me in, she wouldn't hear of me going that far from her protection. My brother would come and visit me instead. The smith he'd been apprenticed to let him make the journey once a year. One day a year for the past eight years, that was all I'd had with Emmet.

"He's going to go absolutely mad," I whispered to myself.

Just imagining the horrified look on Emmet's face when I showed up in Nantic made me walk a little faster.

The sun peering over the ridges of the mountains cut through the chill of the night. The crisp morning air filled my lungs and seemed to banish all the fear that had tried to drown me the day before. The birds swooped through the sky, eager for their breakfast of new spring worms. I longed to fly with them but was happy to settle for using my feet to walk away from Harane.

By the time midday came, I'd started wondering what I would do in Nantic after finding my brother. There wasn't an ink shop in Nantic—Lily had made that clear in the many times she'd bragged about being one of the last proper inkers in the region.

I could find work cleaning or cooking. Emmet would know someone who needed help.

Regret tinged my thoughts of all the people I hadn't said goodbye to. Karin would be furious and poor Cal heartbroken. But there wasn't enough air left for me to breathe in Harane.

I was so busy wondering if I would be able to stay with Emmet, wherever he was living, that I didn't hear the cart coming up behind me until it was only a hundred feet away.

I stepped to the side of the road as soon as I heard the clinking of the horse's bridle. A man and a woman sat in the front of a merchant's wagon with a little boy sleeping peacefully between them.

Keeping my feet on the grass, I nodded as they approached, ready to let them pass before stepping back onto the dirt. But the man pulled on the reins, stopping his horse.

"Hello there." The man nodded back to me.

"Morning." I tightened my grip on my bag.

"Where are you heading?" the man asked.

I stayed silent for a moment, debating whether or not I should share my destination with strangers. There was really only one option for a person heading north along the mountain road. My aim had to be Nantic. Even if my real destination had been farther away, I'd have to stop there first.

"Nantic," I said.

"That's a long way on foot," the woman said.

"The day is fine." I looked up to the bright, cheery sky. "I'll make good enough time."

The subtle pounding in my feet warned me that tomorrow would be a painful day, but I kept my face pleasant as the woman glanced toward the man.

The man examined me, worrying his lips together, before shrugging to the woman.

"There's space in the back," the woman said. "The horse won't notice the difference, and we're all heading the same direction."

"I really don't—"

"What if you're still on the road when night falls?" the woman cut across me. "I don't want leaving a girl alone on the mountain road on my conscience."

"I can make it before dark," I said. "Thank you, though."

"Being near the trees alone isn't a wise idea at any time of day," the woman said.

I tightened my grip on my bag.

"There are spirits in the trees that will lure you in, girl," the woman whispered.

A laugh bubbled in my throat before I saw the look of fear in the woman's eyes.

"I'll stay on the road," I said. "I promise I won't go near the woods."

The woman leaned toward me, risking toppling out of her seat. "I've heard things in the forest. Rustling and echoes of terrible voices. My life to the gods, I'd not wish my worst enemy near those trees alone."

I had no fear of the woods, but getting to Nantic faster would give me more time to find Emmet before dark, and make it less likely that someone from Harane would come riding up the road and find me.

"That's very kind of you." I gave a curtsy and headed for the back of the wagon.

Crates were stacked along both sides of the back, tied to the rails of the cart with only a thin path cutting down the middle. I hopped up and settled myself between the two rows of goods.

With a click from the man, the horse started forward.

"So what's in Nantic for you?" The woman twisted in her seat to speak to me.

"My brother," I said over the rattle of the wheels and creaking of the crates straining against their ropes. "I'm going to live with him."

"The two of you don't live in the same town?" the man asked.

"He was apprenticed out," I said. "Blacksmith."

"A fine calling." The woman stepped over the back of her seat to perch on a crate facing me. "You must be very proud."

"I suppose."

The more I studied the woman's face, the younger she looked. Closer to my own age than a woman established enough to own a wagon full of goods.

"Your brother couldn't come to collect you himself?" she asked.

"No." I stood to be eye-level with the woman. "The smith only lets him leave Nantic once a year. He came to visit me last month, so he couldn't come to fetch me. He's excited to have me living with him, though."

"It's good to have close families."

"What's your name?" I said. "If you don't mind my asking."

"Nirra." Nirra smiled. "And that's Shem."

"Pleasure." Shem waved over his shoulder.

"I'm Ena." I reached for the woman's hand.

Her calluses rubbed against my palm in places where inking hadn't left its mark.

"Your son," I said, peering over the back of the seat at the child still sleeping soundly, "what's his name?"

"He is a lovely child, isn't he?" Nirra smiled down at him. "We're lucky to have him. How old are you?"

"What?" I leaned against the crates behind me.

"To be traveling on the road alone, it's brave for someone of any age," Shem said. "But you look awfully young to be risking it."

"I'm sixteen, I think," I said. "Maybe fifteen or seventeen."

"What a funny thing not to know." Nirra hopped down from her perch to stand in the narrow aisle with me. Her heel struck one of the crates with a hollow thunk.

"My brother will know." I squinted into the crack of the crate behind Nirra. "I lost track of how old I was when our parents died, but he's older. He'll remember."

A sliver of light came through from the far side of the crate with nothing to block its path.

"What sort of thing do you trade in?" I held the strap of my bag with both hands as I moved toward the back of the cart, peeking into the cracks of each container.

"A bit of everything," Nirra said. "It's the only way to keep our family in food and clothes."

"Are you picking goods up in Nantic?" I'd made my way to the end of the cart. Light filtered freely through those crates as well.

"Oh no," Nirra laughed, "we've quite a load of goods to bargain with."

"Then it seems wrong of me to weigh down your wagon." I edged toward the lip of the cart. "I've no coin to give you and I'll be fine on foot."

"Don't be foolish," Shem said. "We don't want any coins from your pocket, and it's not fit for a girl to be traveling the mountain road alone."

"People could start to think all kinds of horrible things about you," Nirra said. "A girl running away on her own? So many terrible possibilities."

"I'm not afraid to be on my own." I watched the ground passing beneath the cart, wondering how badly I might hurt myself if I jumped. "Honestly, the walking will clear my—"

5

I don't remember the world going black. I don't know exactly how it happened or if I actually managed to jump from the cart.

I was talking, and then I was not.

The world was bright with midday sunlight and my gut filled with distrust, and then slanting shadows covered my face and pain filled my head.

The sounds of the rattling cart hadn't changed, though somehow the noise seemed to surround me, and the rumble of the wheels cut into the back of my skull.

I tried to lift my hands to block my ears, but I couldn't move them. My heart froze for a moment before racing like mad. I tried to reason through how I might have fallen and hurt myself so badly I could no longer move my arms. I fought my surging panic and focused on feeling my fingers.

They were cold. My fingers were cold, and my wrists hurt. Something was pinching them, pinning them to my sides. I strained against whatever held me down. I could flex my muscles, I could move my fingers, but I could not break my bonds.

I tried to call for help, but my lips were already parted around the cloth shoved into my mouth.

Breathe, Ena.

The thought brought me no comfort.

You've got to breathe, you chivving fool.

I'd been on a cart. From the noise, I was still on the cart. I squinted at the shadows above me. It was not the open sky. Boards, worn and weathered, hovered six inches above my face.

Spots danced in my vision as I turned my head to the side. A girl with bright blond hair lay next to me. Terror creased her forehead, and a gag had been shoved into her mouth as well.

Swallowing the sick that soared into my throat, I turned my head the other way.

A brown-haired boy no older than ten lay beside me, his eyes closed and body limp.

One of the cart's wheels struck something on the road. The bang from the impact sent a fresh wave of pain through my head.

My body will not be buried in Harane.

I squeezed my eyes shut, forbidding thoughts of how my life would end.

Twisting my fingers, I felt for my bonds. Metal trapped me in place.

What sort of person would have metal cuffs hidden in the floor of their wagon?

I had heard stories of ghosts stealing travelers from the road and assumed they were only stories. That the man who'd disappeared while riding to Hareford hadn't been stolen by the dead, only decided he didn't like his wife and children anymore and run for some faraway part of Ilbrea.

Perhaps I'd been wrong, and there were living men to blame for the violence pinned upon the dead.

"Whoa." The wheels of the cart slowed at the man's voice.

Shem. It must be Shem.

The girl beside me began breathing more quickly, gasping through her nose.

I tried to make a sound of comfort, anything to keep her from choking on her gag, but could only get a low moan past the fabric in my own mouth.

The cart stopped.

"We should get closer," Nirra said.

"Best not to risk it," Shem said. "We'll meet him in the morning. Until then, I'd rather not be spotted."

"What about Ena?" Nirra said. "We don't know if he'll want her."

The cart shifted, and the swish of footsteps through grass came from the left.

"He's not too picky," Shem said. "We'll get a fair price either way."

"We'd make more selling her to a brothel."

Something hit the ground with a thump.

"Couldn't risk selling her in Nantic," Shem said. "Not with a brother in town and home down the road."

"Might be worth hauling her north. Pretty ones like her are hard to find. Men would pay good gold for her."

I balled my hands into fists to stop them from shaking, even though there was no one but the girl beside me to witness my fear.

"No point in arguing until we know if the Guilds want her," Shem said.

Either the Guilds or unknown men would give them coin for me. I didn't know which would be a worse fate. I didn't think I could survive either.

I looked to the girl beside me. Tears trickled down her cheeks. She looked to be my age, maybe a bit older, and these beasts were going to give her to the Guilds.

I didn't know what for. It didn't matter.

Anger singed through my fear.

I tried to move my feet, wanting to kick up into the boards above me. Metal cut into my ankles. I unfurled my fists and lay my palms flat against the rough wood beneath me. I lifted my fingers and smacked my hands against the boards as hard as I could.

The movement only made a small thud, but it was better than nothing. I struck the wood again, ignoring the pain as the metal cut into my wrists.

Thud. Thud. Thud. Thud.

I pounded against the boards until the movement outside stopped.

"Is someone awake in there?" Shem's voice came from only a few feet away.

I took a deep breath and screamed against my gag.

"Better to be quiet," Shem hushed. "Just close your eyes and sleep."

I screamed again, smacking my hands against the wood as hard as I could.

Footsteps thumped to the back of the wagon.

"What are you doing?" Shem said.

"We're not going to be able to sleep through that," Nirra said.

The rasp of metal sliding against metal came the moment before the ceiling lifted away with a great creak.

I blinked against the moonlight as a silhouette towered over me.

"I should have known you'd be the one making a fuss," Nirra said.

I yelled all the curses in my mind through my gag.

"Be quiet or I'll have to bash your head again," Nirra said.

I smacked my hands against the wood.

"Why are you so reluctant?" Nirra stepped down from the lip of the wagon into the hollowed out bottom where they'd stored me and the others. "Are you a sorci running from the Guilds?"

I glared up at her.

"Are you carrying a fatherless babe and running from the wrath of the Guilds?"

I balled my hands into fists, wishing to the stars I could tear the skin right off Nirra's foul face.

"Are you a fool running alone on the mountain road to your brother?" Nirra leaned down so her face was only a foot above mine. "You don't seem naïve enough for that to be the truth."

I raised my eyebrows, daring her to pull the gag from my mouth.

Nirra looked to the girl next to me. "She was an easy one to spot. Sitting alone in a tavern, telling tales of the husband who would be coming to meet her. How far did you think you could run before your belly gave you away?"

The girl gave a shuddering breath as tears streamed down her face.

"The Guilds pay three gold coins for turning in a fool carrying a bastard." Nirra ran her finger along the girl's cheek. "They're going to put you on a boat and ship you off to Ian Ayres. Too bad the man you spread your legs for didn't love you enough to marry you. Now your child will be born on the island the demons created. Cruel of the Guilds to hide fatherless children in such a vile place. I can't complain, though. Your indiscretion is pure profit for me."

The girl coughed on her gag as she whimpered.

I slapped my hands against the floor again.

"What?" Nirra said.

"Keep her quiet," Shem said.

I screamed against my gag.

Nirra slapped me hard across the face.

Stars danced through my vision as I smacked my hands on the boards again and screamed.

"What, Ena?" Nirra said. "Are you hoping I'll bargain your freedom with your brother? I doubt a blacksmith can pay enough."

I screamed again.

Nirra yanked the gag from my mouth.

I gulped down fresh air.

"What did you have to do that for?" Shem said.

The wagon shifted as he stepped up onto the back.

"What do you want to tell me?" Nirra leaned over me. "That we're monsters? That we can't sell you? You deserve your freedom? Oh, I know, your brother will track us down? He'll tear up all of Ilbrea searching for his beloved sister?"

"I don't know how you think he'd find me," I said. "I was heading for Nantic on foot. Who could have guessed I'd end up under the floor of a wagon?"

Nirra laughed. "Clever enough to realize that, but not to keep your mouth shut about it?"

"Clever enough to steal people on the road, but not to make the most coin off them?" I mimicked Nirra's high, rolling laugh. "I never thought I'd be kidnapped, but if I had imagined it, I think I would have pictured you a bit smarter."

Pain shot through my face as Nirra slapped me again.

"If you don't want to make the most of your efforts in kidnapping me, on your own head be it. Put the gag back in and go about your business." I opened my mouth wide, forcing my features to relax as I waited for the fabric to stifle the flow of air into my mouth.

Nirra glared down at me.

"Shut her up and let's pitch the tent," Shem said. "I'm tired, Nirra."

I locked eyes with Nirra, waiting for her to shove the gag back into my mouth.

"Nirra." Shem stepped down into the bottom of the wagon. He reached for the cloth in her grip, but she pulled her hand away. "We'll get plenty of coin for her."

I allowed myself the comfort of a grin as Nirra looked slowly to Shem.

"He's right," I said. "I'm young and pretty. A brothel won't mind giving you a few coins. If you're doing well enough, there's no point in ruining your system of commerce. I'll talk to whatever brothel matron you sell me to. I can be patient."

"What will you tell her?" Nirra knelt beside me. "What secret are you so desperate to share, Ena?"

Shem huffed, worrying his lips together so it looked like he might bite them off.

"Shem's not interested," I said. "Best to shut me up and pitch your tent."

"Shem, take care of the tent."

Shem opened his mouth like he might argue, but a withering glare from Nirra sent him back to chewing his lips as he climbed down from the wagon.

"Now it's just us girls," Nirra said. "What secret do you have that would save you from your fate?"

"I'm worth far more than anyone will pay for my body," I said.

The sounds of Shem's movement stopped.

"There are those who will pay a fist of gold coins for my freedom," I whispered so Shem couldn't hear.

"And who would that be?" Nirra said. "Do you have a fancy Guilded lover waiting for you in Nantic?"

"No." I smiled as though I were trying to drink in the moonlight. "It's the ghosts of the mountains who will pay for my safety."

6

Every child of Harane grew up knowing the stories of the ghosts in the eastern mountains   souls of long dead bandits claiming the life and treasure of any fool who ventured into their territory. Most villagers still believed the stories even when their hair had turned a wintery gray.

The travelers who passed through Harane would speak in low voices of the lives lost to the spirits of the mountains. Grown men had been brought to tears by their fear of the bandit ghosts. Even the Guilded soldiers would do whatever it took to stay out of the great forests that covered the mountains' slopes.

I, however, knew those stories were wrong.

A certain childlike glee filled my heart as I watched Nirra's face shift from disbelief, to greed, to fear.

"You don't think I would be fool enough to wander along the mountain road if I were frightened of the ones who wait in the woods?" I asked.

"I'm not a child," Nirra said. "Don't try to sell me on scary stories of the Black Bloods haunting the woods."

"Black Bloods?" I laughed. "The dead don't care what names we call them. They care for the gold they hoard away from the grasp of the Guilds, and the living folk who help them grow their fortunes."

"Why would the dead need money?" Shem asked.

"Why do the living hoard jewels?" I said.

"And how are you supposed to help them?" Nirra asked.

"I can show you if you like." I winked up at her.

"Just tell her." Shem leapt back up onto the wagon, shaking the boards beneath me.

My mind raced, trying to think through a reasonable explanation for how I could be of use to a mythical band of ghosts.

You will not panic.

"She's run out of lies to tell," Shem said.

"There are things more important than gold to the ghosts," I said. "Men."

I waited for either of them to speak, but Nirra just watched me like a child enthralled in a story while Shem chewed his chivving lips.

"The souls of men." I spoke in a low voice, the way Emmet had when we were little and he wanted to frighten me. "The spirits of thousands of men wander through the mountains, free of the Guilds and their laws. They have their woods and gold, but what they want is more men to join their ranks."

"Why would they want that?" Nirra said.

"Because one day, they will come out of the woods and destroy the Guilds." I looked up to the stars. "I deliver them men. They pay me from their treasures. That is how I serve the dead."

"But you were going to live with your brother," Shem said.

"There are more men in Nantic than in Harane," I said. "The ghosts are willing to pay, no matter how many I deliver. Why shouldn't I bring them more?"

"It's not true, Nirra," Shem said. "It can't be."

"How many gold pieces would you want from them for my freedom? Ten? Twenty?" I held my breath, watching as Nirra's greed overwhelmed her reason.

"Your freedom would cost thirty gold pieces," Nirra said.

A shock zapped through my veins at the mere thought of such a treasure, let alone the idea of it being traded for an orphan from Harane.

"Done." I relaxed on the boards as though the deal had been finished and it was my time to sleep.

Nirra stood, planting her hands on her hips and looking to the sky.

"Is the money just supposed to appear now?" Shem said. "Should I start checking my pockets?"

"Don't be daft," I said. "If you want the gold, I'll have to go and fetch it from the ghosts."

"And we should just let you wander in?" Nirra laughed.

"Of course not," I said. "You can come in with me and get it for yourself."

Shem laid a hand on Nirra's shoulder.

"Tie my wrists, and I'll take you in," I said. "Both of you are welcome to come. Though I've never led a man in and had him come back alive. I don't know how the ghosts will feel about that."

"Tie her up," Nirra said.

"What?" Shem pulled his hand away.

"Unlock her, and tie her up," Nirra said.

"For a ghost story?" Shem said.

"They aren't just stories, and you know it," Nirra spat. "There are things in those woods even the Guilds don't dare test. A sorcerer wouldn't be brave enough to venture into the mountains."

"So we shouldn't—"

"We have never gained from fear," Nirra sneered. "Now unlock the Black Blood's girl."

Nirra jumped down off the back of the wagon, and Shem swore to himself as he unlocked my wrists.

Part of me wanted to kick Shem the moment my feet were

free, but I could hear the grass swishing as Nirra paced at the back of the cart.

Shem slipped the iron key into his pocket.

I looked to the blond girl. Fear filled her tear-soaked face.

Shem grabbed my arm and yanked me to my feet.

The night swayed around me.

I gasped and tipped forward, falling onto Shem.

"Careful now." Shem grabbed me around the waist, holding me tight.

I quickened my breath. "What under the stars did you do to my head?" I slumped against him, slipping my hand into his pocket.

"I'll do worse to you if you don't get off him and climb down here," Nirra said.

"Give her a moment." Shem steadied me, his hands drifting up to my ribs. "You're the one who wanted to unlock her after all."

"Just tie her up." Nirra stomped toward the front of the wagon.

"Are you going to come with me?" I tucked my hand into my own pocket as Shem jumped from the back of the wagon.

He reached up to lift me down.

"No, he will not." Nirra reappeared, a lantern in one hand and a rope in the other. "You and I are going to chase your Black Bloods through the forest. If I don't come out with my thirty gold pieces, I'll sell you to the foulest people in the market."

I shoved away the shiver that threatened to betray me.

"Come on then." I held my hands out in front of me, ready to be tied.

I studied the silhouette of the mountains in the moonlight as she knotted my wrists painfully together.

They'd stopped their wagon on the western side of the road, keeping as far away from the mountains as they could.

I looked north toward Nantic. There wasn't a glimmer of light to be seen.

"Walk," Nirra ordered.

"Eager for your gold?" I said. "Shem, if you hear noises in the forest, don't follow them."

"What?" Shem froze.

"Once the ghosts know you're out here, they might try to lure you in for themselves." I didn't look back at the wagon or at Shem as I walked toward the mountains.

I wanted to scream to the blond girl that I would come back for her, but with Nirra holding the end of the rope that bound me, I wasn't sure I would survive that long.

A dull ache throbbed through my feet and head with every step. The tall grass clung to my skirt, as though begging me not to go into the forest. I wanted to sink into the grass and hide, but I'd given up my other choices when I'd chosen to stake my life on a ghost story.

There were other lies I could have told. I could have promised my brother would pay my ransom. I didn't know if Emmet had any coin, but I was certain he would try to help.

Cal would have paid every coin he had for my freedom. His family owned the only tavern in Harane, so they might've even been able to come up with enough to satisfy Nirra's greed.

But like the chivving slitch of a fool I was, I looked to the mountains for protection.

The eastern mountains were pleased to claim a fool's life, but there were no ghosts involved in the deaths of those who strayed into the woods. There were beasts who roamed the night, cliffs that would crumble sooner than let you climb them, and so much land you could wander for a hundred years and never find your way back home.

The people of Ilbrea feared the mountains, so the solitude they provided had become my refuge when Lily took me in. The place I could run when nightmares threatened to swallow me even during my waking hours. A shelter when the Guilds' soldiers came down the mountain road.

I'd spent days on end roaming the slopes, foraging for plants to aid in Lily's remedies and inks. The mountains had become the best protection I had, but I couldn't conjure ghosts, or thirty gold coins from the shadows of the forest.

The grass disappeared as we stepped into the cover of the trees. I took a deep breath, letting the damp, crisp air fill my lungs.

"Well," Nirra said.

"Well what?" I turned to her.

The lantern light playing across her face made her look even younger. She was practically a child, and somehow she'd ended up selling people to the Guilds.

How did you get here?

The question balanced on my tongue.

"Are you going to call them?" Nirra asked.

"I don't call them," I laughed. "They aren't pet dogs. I have to go to them."

I tramped through the trees until the rope became too taut for me to continue.

"Would you like me to go alone?" I turned to Nirra. "I'm happy to wander off into the mountains on my own."

"What do you take me for? A fool?" Nirra stomped after me, her lantern held high.

7

I wish I were closer to Harane.

The thought kept echoing in my head as I climbed through the forest. If I'd been closer to Harane, I would have known exactly which slopes led to where. But the mountains' secrets were foreign to me this far north.

I could tell by the growth of the trees how much rock was in the soil. The moss whispered which direction we were traveling without my having to see the stars for guidance. But I didn't know which path led to safety and which to the darkness of an animal's den.

I wish I were closer to Harane.

"Where are they?" Nirra said. Branches cracked under her feet as she trailed behind me, gripping the end of the rope that tied me in one hand and her lantern in the other.

"I've never met them here, so I have to find where they hunt." I cut north, using my bound hands to lift the front of my skirt as I scrambled up a steep incline.

"Slow down." Nirra yanked on the rope.

I swayed, catching my balance. "You've got to make up your mind. Do you want me to find them quickly, or walk slowly?"

"Don't make me regret bringing you in here," Nirra said. "You are my prisoner until I have gold in my hands. You'd do well to remember that."

I gave a deep sigh. "Fine. I will climb more slowly."

My legs burned as I took the slope at a crawling pace. A set of crumbling boulders met us at the top of the rise. I took a long breath, scenting the wind.

"Do you smell it?" I whispered.

"What?" Nirra sniffed the air.

"Decay." I turned on the spot, examining the terrain.

"Is that them? Do the ghosts smell like death?"

"Ghosts don't smell like anything. It's the bodies of the men they've claimed that stink of rot."

Leaves rustled to the north of us, swishing in a pattern that had nothing to do with the wind.

"What's that?" Nirra stepped closer to me.

"Animal." I dug my nails into my palms, willing my heart to remain steady. "Wolf, maybe."

I sent a silent plea to whatever god would be willing to listen to a chivving slitch of a fool who'd wandered into the woods after dark that whatever animal was prowling wouldn't be hungry.

The rustling of leaves came closer, and my fear changed. Perhaps it wasn't an animal come looking for its supper. Perhaps there were real bandits living in the woods and I'd just wandered my way into becoming the captive of someone far worse than Nirra.

"Come on." I sidestepped so Nirra could walk next to me as I cut along the top of the rise. "If it's an animal, don't run. You'll never outpace a beast in the woods. The best thing you can do is climb and hope they don't have claws sharp enough to follow."

"Where are the ghosts?" Nirra whispered.

"I think I can feel them."

The ridge in front of us had been worn away, torn apart by a patch of rocks as though a giant had scuffed his heel through the dirt.

"Watch your feet. The ghosts have never cared for easy terrain." I felt like a fool giving such a warning, but Nirra picked her way carefully across the rocks, testing each step.

A thin tree struggled for life at the edge of the rock slide. I leapt the last few feet, catching hold of the trunk between my hands.

"What are you doing?" Nirra said.

"The tree is warm." I tightened my grip. "It's a good sign."

"Shouldn't Black Bloods leave everything cold?"

"Not at all. Come feel for yourself."

She stepped up behind me, reaching for the tree.

I took a deep breath and kicked back as hard as I could.

She screamed as my boot met her knee.

The rocks clacked as she tumbled away, the rope still in her grip.

I clung to the tree, gritting my teeth as her full weight yanked on the tether. The awful pain lasted only a moment before the rope slipped from Nirra's grip, and she slid to the base of the slope.

I took off running through the trees. The rope trailed behind me, catching on fallen branches. I slowed my pace enough to gather the rope over my shoulder but didn't dare stop.

The shadows of the trees made every boulder seem like a monster waiting to pounce. The rustling of the wind through the leaves was the Black Bloods come to kill me for taking advantage of their legend.

Cutting up another slope, I ran farther into the mountains.

I'd never been brave enough to stray into the forest at night. I knew the ghosts were a lie, but animals with sharp claws were very real and could easily kill me. I wanted to take my own advice. Climb a tree and wait for the safety of sunrise, but my hands were bound, and I couldn't risk staying put.

I reached the top of the rise. In the faint moonlight, all I could see to the east was more mountains without a hint of sanctuary. I ran south along the ridgeline back toward the wagon. It wasn't until I reached the edge of a cliff that I finally stopped.

Sweat slicked my neck as I gulped down air. My arms burned from carrying the weight of the rope. I scanned the forest below, searching for any glimmer of Nirra's lantern. I couldn't remember if it had gone out when she'd fallen. I strained my ears, listening for any hint of her chasing me.

Nothing.

Just the wind and my own breathing.

I knelt by the edge of the cliff, squinting at the knots that bound my wrists. I bit into the rope, pulling with my teeth.

"I wish I had a knife," I mumbled into the knot.

The rope gave a bit but not enough for me to wriggle free.

"No use wishing for things you can't have." I patted along the ground, searching for something I could shove into the knot.

Every heartbeat felt like an eternity as I twisted my hands, using a stick to pry the knot loose. The skin on my wrists tore, but I didn't care. Nothing mattered but breaking free.

I'd led Nirra on a rambling enough path I didn't think she'd be able to find her way to edge of the woods too quickly. And I'd run far enough she shouldn't have been able to follow. If she'd gotten up at all.

I shoved my slim shred of sympathy down as the rope came loose and I managed to drag my hands free of their binding.

I rubbed warmth into my fingers as I stared down over the cliff. It wasn't high, only twenty-five odd feet. I looked back the way I'd come.

There was still no hint of Nirra, but retreating toward her seemed more dangerous than risking the cliff.

Glancing up to the stars, I begged for their mercy before kicking my feet over the ledge.

My pulse slowed as I lowered my body. There was nothing

between death and life but me and the rocks I clung to. No ghosts or kidnappers could interfere with my fate.

The pain in my wrists faded as the muscles in my arms began to burn.

The cliff was harder to cling to than a tree, but no worse than finding handholds on the side of a stone house. The movement was familiar and comforting to me. Wind kissed the back of my neck, drying my sweat and easing my fear.

The descent took time, testing each foothold, carefully keeping my skirt from wrapping around my ankles, hoping I was making proper sense of the shadows.

Too soon, I reached the bottom and was back on solid ground. The reality of being trapped in the woods came crashing back, crushing my chest with the weight of it.

I took one more moment, listening for sounds in the darkness—

Nothing.

—then started down the mountain.

8

The moonlight shone on the tall grass as it swayed in the night wind. I'd never seen the sea, but from the stories I'd been told, the scene looked like waves of silver luring travelers into a fairy kingdom.

Only it wasn't a fairy waiting for me in the middle of the silver sea.

Shem sat on top of the wagon, lantern by his side as he stared at the woods.

She hasn't come back.

I tamped down the guilt that rolled in my stomach and locked my gaze on the back of the cart.

I couldn't think of a plan to lure Shem away. Not one that wouldn't end with my being caught. I pressed my fists to my temples, trying to squeeze my exhausted thoughts into a reasonable order. Pain pulsed in the back of my head where Nirra had hit me.

"Chivving cact of a slitching slug." I knelt, searching the ground around me.

A night bird called from the north. I looked toward the sound. My fingers stopped their scouring of the dirt.

I could head north. Stick to the trees. Find a sturdy one to climb and wait for morning. If Nirra hadn't found me yet, I doubted she would be able to track me before dawn. I'd wait for daylight and keep to the mountains until I made it to Nantic. I'd never have to see Nirra or Shem again. It would be like the whole thing had never happened.

I closed my eyes, picturing the tear-streaked face of the blond girl, wondering if I could survive her haunting my dreams for the rest of my days.

My nightmares were already more than I could bear.

I tried not to think as I dug through the dirt to find my weapons. Knowing all the ways I might get myself killed wouldn't make acting any easier. When I'd found a stone larger than my fist and a stick thicker than my arm, I crept north to be level with the wagon.

I pressed my back to the trunk of a wide tree.

"You are not a coward, Ena Ryeland."

I raised my stick and struck it against the side of the tree.

Crack.

The sound shook my teeth. Something scurried away in the nearby brush.

I held my breath, waiting for Nirra to come bolting through the trees, ready to kill me.

Crack.

I struck the tree again. Tiny bits of bark shattered from its surface.

A sound did come this time, but not from the forest. A creaking carried from across the road as Shem jumped down from the wagon, lantern held high.

Crack.

He walked to the center of the road.

Crack.

"Nirra?" Shem squinted toward the woods. "Nirra, is that you?"

Crack.

"Nirra, I've never once thought you were funny."

Crack.

"Ena?" Shem crept to the eastern side of the road. "I'm not the fool Nirra is. I don't believe in your ghost stories."

Crack.

The stick began to splinter.

"Come out of the woods right now, and I might consider taking pity on you."

Crack.

"I'm tired of your chivving games."

Shem strode straight toward me. He moved his hand to his belt, pulling a long knife from a sheath hidden by his coat.

Trusting the shadows, I slunk backward, away from the tree I'd bashed the bark off of.

"There are worse places than brothels for a petal whore like you," Shem spat.

I heaved the stone with all my might, launching it at the brush the small creature had fled.

Shem smiled. "You're going to wish you'd stayed with Nirra."

I held my breath as he stalked forward raising his knife. He leaned into the brush, his blade glinting in the lantern light.

"Ena, where are you?"

I lunged toward him.

He turned at the sound of my swishing skirt. His eyes grew wide as I swung for his head, but he wasn't quick enough to strike with his knife. The stick broke in half with a great crack, and Shem fell to the ground.

I took a ragged breath, waiting for him to spring to his feet and slash his knife at me. But as blood blossomed on his forehead, he made no move to reach for the blade that lay by his hand.

My whole body trembled as I kicked the knife away from him. But still he didn't move.

Glass fell from a broken pane in his lantern as I lifted it, and he said nothing.

I kept my gaze locked on his face as I bent down, fumbling for his knife. The blade sliced my finger before I found the hilt.

I backed away, feeling my path with my toes. It wasn't until I was twenty feet from him that I dared to turn and run for the cart.

The ghosts of the eastern mountains might as well have been chasing me as I sprinted across the road. I stopped at the back of the wagon, studying the shadows of the forest for movement before setting the lantern down.

I waited a breath, then another.

"Are you awake in there?" I spoke as loudly as I dared.

Two muffled voices answered me.

I ran my hands along the back of the cart, searching for a catch. My fingers met cold metal—a slide lock painted brown to blend with the rest of the cart. I pushed the bolt aside and heaved the wood up. The center slats between the two rows of crates tilted. Another round of muffled cries came from the darkness below.

"Hold on." I tucked the knife into my pocket and picked up the lantern, giving one last glance toward the forest before climbing into the back of the wagon and heaving the boards all the way up.

I bent low to peer into the dark corners of the wooden prison.

The blond girl and brown-haired boy stared wide-eyed at me.

"We have to move quickly." I knelt beside the girl, fumbling in my pocket for the key I'd stolen what seemed like a lifetime ago. My fingers sliced on the knife again, but I didn't dare waste time checking the damage. "I'll unlock you, then you unlock him. Can you do that?"

The girl nodded.

Please let the key work.

I fitted the iron key into the lock and turned. The cuff opened with a dull click.

The girl winced as she lifted her arm to pull the gag from her mouth.

"Where are they?" The words rasped in her throat as though she hadn't spoken in a week.

"In the woods, but I don't know when they'll come back." I unlocked her other wrist before moving on to the bar that pinned her feet to the floor.

"We have to get out of here." The girl gasped as she sat up, her eyes losing focus from the movement.

"The little boy, where is he?" I pressed the iron key into her hand.

"The front of the wagon." The girl rolled to her hands and knees, panting from the effort. "The man might've moved him to their tent. I don't know."

The brown-haired boy screamed against his gag.

"Get him unlocked and get the back of the wagon closed." I leapt to my feet.

"I've got you." The girl crawled toward him. "I won't leave you like this."

I jumped down from the cart. My knees buckled beneath me. Stones dug into my palms as I caught myself in the grass.

No shadows came charging out of the mountains as I struggled to my feet. I grabbed the lantern, holding the light up to peer into the front of the wagon. The little boy wasn't sleeping on the seat as I'd seen him before.

A tent had been set up nearby, with the horse tied beside it. I didn't like the idea of going into the canvas. The thought of not being able to see the world around me sent my pulse racing so fast I thought I might die.

Setting the lantern by the tent, I pulled the knife from my pocket and flung the flap aside.

Two cots had been set up. The child had been left tied up in the grass between them.

He looked even smaller than he had when he'd been nestled between Nirra and Shem.

"Wake up." I put the knife back into my pocket. "Boy, wake up."

The child didn't stir.

"Please." I knelt beside him, feeling his face for warmth. "You can't do this to me."

The grass rustled outside the tent.

I snatched the boy up, cradling him to my chest.

"I don't know how to hook a horse to a cart." A young boy's voice came through the canvas.

"I can do it."

The horse gave a sigh at the blond girl's words.

My legs screamed as I stood and ducked back out of the tent.

The boy from the wagon lifted the lantern, holding it high as the girl fastened the horse to the cart.

"Are we leaving?" The boy's face was pale. Raw skin from the gag shone around his mouth.

"We're taking the cart and heading north." I hoped I sounded like I wasn't terrified. "They won't be able to catch up to us, and once we're in Nantic, we can get help."

"Help from who?" The girl froze, her hands grasping the horse's reins.

"I…"

"I can't go to the Guilds," the boy said before I could begin to think of who might be able to help us. "If they find out what I am, I'll be sent to the Sorcerers Guild. I'll spend the rest of my life locked up in a stone tower serving the Lady Sorcerer."

"I can't go to them either," the girl said.

"We'll figure it out once we're on the road." I ran for the wagon, lifting the child onto the seat before climbing up.

The girl scrambled up beside me. "Have you driven a cart?"

I shook my head.

"I can." She tightened her grip on the reins.

The boy stood in front of the horse, a kind of terror in his eyes I'd only seen a few times before.

"We've got to go," I said.

"Promise"—the boy glanced toward the trees—"promise you won't turn me in. No matter how much gold the Guilds offer you."

"I promise," the girl said.

"I'd rather eat a dagger than give anything to the Guilds." I reached for the boy's hand. "I promise I won't give you to the golden monsters."

Wrinkles formed on the boy's brow.

"We can't be here if they come out of the woods," I said. "Please, just trust me."

The boy nodded and took my non-bloodied hand.

The girl clicked for the horse to move before the boy had both feet in the cart.

I kept my gaze locked on the trees where I'd left Shem for as long as I could. No shadow emerged from the woods to chase us.

9

I didn't know how far from Nantic we'd been when Nirra and Shem had stopped the cart. I hoped we were still heading for Nantic and hadn't somehow passed through while I was locked up and unconscious under the floor of the wagon.

My neck prickled even knowing the compartment where we'd been hidden was still traveling with us. How many others had been chained below and sold to the Guilds? How many times had those monsters traveled through Harane, searching for victims?

We didn't speak for the first hour on the road. I don't know if all of us were too tired or just too afraid speaking might summon Nirra and Shem from the forest still looming over us to the east.

The shadowed shapes of houses began dotting the darkness as we traveled farther north. A barn had been built close enough to the road I could have grazed its peeling paint with my fingers.

Before I'd managed to force myself to talk, the first glimmer of lantern light shone in the distance.

"Is that Nantic?" the girl asked.

"I hope so," I said.

"I"—the boy took a shuddering breath—"I can't go to Nantic."

"Why not?" the girl said.

The boy wrapped his arms around his middle as though he were going to be ill.

"Are you from Nantic?" I asked.

He shook his head. "They found me in the south."

"Then what's wrong with Nantic?" I asked. "Even if you're…if you were born with magic—"

"Born a sorcerer." The boy stared into my eyes.

There was a glimmer of something within them. Beyond his fear and determination. A spark of something I couldn't quite name.

My heart soared into my throat. My fingers itched to reach for the knife still hidden in my pocket.

"I won't hurt you." The boy's face crumpled. "I've never hurt anyone. Not really. Might've scared a few people on accident, but I've never caused anyone real harm. I'm chivving awful with magic.

"Most of the time it's the best I can manage just to keep it pressed down where no one will notice it. I can hardly ever do magic when I mean to. I'd been trying to get out of my cuffs whenever the stuff they gave me to sleep wore off. I tried for days and couldn't break free."

"I'm sorry." I folded my hands in my lap. "I've never met someone with magic in their blood."

"Because the sorcerers take them all." The boy gripped his stomach even tighter. "They take them north to the capital, to the Sorcerers Tower in Ilara. You pass through their stone gates, and you're never free again."

"I'm sorry," the girl said. "It sounds like a terrible fate, but I don't know what it has to do with Nantic."

"The sorcerers are traveling," the boy said, "out hunting for more children with magic. Shem said they were going to be in Nantic. They were taking me there for the bounty."

I scrubbed my hands over my face. "Will the sorcerers know you're magic if no one hands you over?"

"I don't know," the boy said. "I've never met anyone else like me. I don't know if there's a spell or if they can scent me..."

"Stop the cart," I said.

"But we're almost there," the girl said.

"Just stop the cart."

The girl shook her head, but pulled back on the reins all the same.

"Where do you need to go?" I looked to the girl.

"What?" Her face paled.

"If you were in a tavern when they caught you, you must have been heading somewhere," I said.

The girl looked to the glimmering lights in the distance.

"Were you trying to get to the child's father?" I asked. "Is there some safe place you were heading for?"

"No." A tear rolled down the girl's cheek. "My mother found out about the baby. She was going to turn me in. Said it was better to have me shipped to Ian Ayres than to have the stain of a bastard on the family. So I picked up and ran. I didn't have any sort of a plan besides getting away from her."

"There's a crossroad just north of Nantic," I said. "You can cut through the city then go west, toward the sea. I don't know what you'll find that way, but at least you won't be here. The child, why did they have him?" I looked down to the little boy who slept soundly at my feet.

"I think he must have magic in him, too," the boy said. "They had him before they took me. They were careful to keep him asleep all the time. I don't know why else they would have gone to the trouble."

"You'll take him with you," I said. "Promise you'll keep him safe."

"I'll do my best," the boy said.

I nodded, trying not to think of the hundred horrible things that could happen to them.

"Should I stay with them?" the girl asked.

"That's your choice," I said. "But I have to go to Nantic. My brother's there. I'd say he'd help you—"

"It's too much to ask anyone to protect you from the Guilds." The girl squeezed my hand.

Her fingers felt so delicate around mine, like she was nothing more than spun glass teetering on the edge of being smashed by the world.

"I'll get out here." I ignored the pain in my legs as I jumped down from the cart. "It'll be better if you go straight through town without stopping."

"Right." The girl stared at me as though searching for something else to say.

"Be safe." I nodded to them.

"What's your name?" the boy said.

"Doesn't matter," I said.

"But you saved us," he said. "Shouldn't I know who to thank the gods for sending?"

"No." I gave them the best smile I could. "Just hold on to your freedom. Now go."

The girl clicked to the horse, and the cart rumbled away.

I waited on the side of the road until the dust settled behind the wagon's wheels.

There was a void in my chest. I didn't know those people—I couldn't have told you the color of the babe's eyes, I'd never even seen them open—but I stood alone in the dark, feeling utterly hollow. They could all be dead by sunrise, and I would never know.

"They have a cart," I said to myself as I forced one foot in front of the other. "They have a horse and each other. They would have been sold if you hadn't unlocked them. They are better off than when you found them."

The weight of the knife hung heavy in my pocket.

I should have given it to them.

I wished I could have protected them, ferried them someplace far away where they would be safe from the wrath of the Guilds.

There is no such place.

Even if I had managed to sneak them to Lily, their fate wouldn't have changed.

"Just get to Emmet. You cannot save the world, Ena Ryeland. Just get to your chivving brother."

I kept my gaze fixed on the lights of Nantic even as exhaustion dragged on my limbs, threatening to topple me as I walked.

My fingers burned from cold, my throat from thirst.

"Get to Emmet."

The lights became clearer as I neared the town.

A line of posts had been planted along the road leading up to a tavern with a big blue sign out front.

The Traveler's Rest

I longed for a chance to sleep safely in a bed, but the few coins I'd had when I'd left Harane had been taken by Nirra and Shem. I'd been too afraid to spend time searching for my bag in the tent and hadn't thought of looking for it in the wagon.

I wasn't sorry.

The others needed coin more than I needed a warm bed.

I walked past the lanterns leading up to the tavern and into the town proper. The windows in most of the houses were dark. Here and there, a candle burned in a window, though I didn't know who the flames might have been calling home.

My shoulders tensed as I moved past the houses and into the part of town where shops took over. A few sounds of life carried from the shadows of the stables, and the high clunk of wood being stacked came from behind a bakery.

The buildings around me grew taller and the road narrower as I reached the center of Nantic. I hadn't seen a sign for a black-smith. Honestly, I didn't actually know the name of the shop where my brother worked, let alone which corner of town it might be in.

"Funny thing to realize now, you fool." I stepped into a narrow alley beside a dress shop. I pressed my forehead to the rough stone of the building. The world swayed as I shut my eyes. "Just find a place to rest until morning."

The alley was dark enough to hide me, but even with the knife in my pocket, I didn't feel safe sleeping where I could easily be snatched up again.

I ran my hands along the stones of the dress shop. The mason had done a good enough job keeping the building stable, but he hadn't packed the mortar in to make the walls smooth. There were two stories on top of the shop. The dressmaker and a mess of other workers probably lived up there. I rubbed my hands on my skirt, hoping the seamstresses were sound sleepers, and started to climb.

The cuts on my fingers stung and my legs shook as I pulled myself up step by step.

I allowed myself the comfort of a smile as I imagined what Emmet would say when I told him I'd spent my first night in Nantic sleeping on top of a shop.

My arms trembled as I dragged myself onto the slanted roof and crawled behind the chimney to curl up and sleep.

10

The pounding of hooves echoed through my dreams, but I was too exhausted for fear to pull me from my slumber. Sounds flitted in and out of being until a voice joined the dark images, cutting through the fog and dragging me back into the world.

I opened my eyes and blinked, trying to figure out why there would be stone so close to my face.

My neck ached as I lifted my head to examine the blackened chimney. A faint warmth still carried through the rocks I'd slept huddled against.

"Step back," a man shouted down below. "All of you step back. The sorcerer is coming to address the people of Nantic, and by the Guilds' orders you've got to give her a bit of room."

I pushed myself to my hands and knees, biting back a gasp as pain shot through my body.

"We will have order while the sorcerer speaks," the man shouted over the grumbling of the crowd. "Every one of you will listen respectfully, or you will be reminded how a citizen of Ilbrea should show their gratitude to the Guilds."

Inching forward, I peeked over the pitch of the roof to peer at the street below.

A hundred people had packed together in front of a building four shops down, facing a line of soldiers wearing black uniforms.

I hadn't noticed the seven-pointed star in front of the building the night before. Now, with the sun up, the golden crest of the Guilds glinted in the light, hanging above a sign that read *Scribes of Ilbrea*.

I pulled myself along the roof, trying to get a better look at the crowd that had gathered below.

A tall soldier with graying hair stood on the porch of the scribes' shop, glaring at the common folk surrounding him.

The people didn't look too pleased to be standing in front of a line of soldiers either. They shifted their weight and glanced up and down the street. A ring of empty space separated the people from the porch, as though the barren patch the soldier had demanded had been taken up by some invisible force.

The door of the shop opened, and a woman in purple robes stepped out. The bright color of her robes, the way her dark, shining hair had been pinned perfectly back, and the way she gazed down at the people around her, all combined to make the sorcerer mesmerizing.

But there was something in the way a smile curved her lips that terrified me.

"People of Nantic"—the sorcerer's voice carried easily over the silent crowd—"I am pleased you have ventured out to see me on this beautiful morning. It is rare for sorcerers to leave Ilara. Our duty is to aid Ilbrea. We help our country, and the Guilds who govern us all, best by remaining in our stronghold. Perfecting the magic that protects each one of you."

The sorcerer held her hand out in front of her. A tiny glimmer appeared in her palm.

The light was beautiful, like a fairy had been birthed in her hand. Before I could blink, the spark changed, growing into a pillar of purple fire ten feet tall.

The crowd gasped and backed away as the flames leapt toward the sky.

"Our magic provides safety to all who live in Ilbrea." She threw the fire into the air. The flames morphed into a giant firebird that flew in circles above her head, screeching at the crowd. "The strength of the sorcerers protects Ilbrea from those who would attack us."

She clapped her hands. A boom that shook the air blasted over the people, stealing my breath as it shot pain into my ears.

"We have the power to heal." The sorcerer spoke over the cries of the crowd. She raised a hand high over her head and snapped her fingers.

The pain in my ears vanished. I gasped, clinging to the top of the roof, wanting nothing more than to run away, but unable to force my body to move.

"The gifts sorcerers are born with are powerful, and valuable. But imagine"—she wiped her hand across the sky. The flaming bird transformed into a dark cloud that pressed down upon the crowd, shrouding them in a thick haze—"what these powers would be like in the hands of an untrained child? How much damage could one misled individual cause?

"What could a child do in a fit of temper? How quickly could they destroy you, your home, your family? I do not show you these things to frighten you. It is not the aim of the Sorcerers Guild to have anyone fear our magic. I have shown you my power so you will understand what is at stake."

The haze cleared from the street. The common folk were still there, but they seemed to have changed, lessened. Their shoulders were hunched in fear. The few faces I could see had paled.

"I am traveling through Ilbrea, seeking children who have been born with magic," the sorcerer said. "Not to harm them, but to train them. To give them a home where they can grow and thrive. Where they can be kept safe while they learn to protect Ilbrea."

The door of the shop opened. The crowd backed away, pressing each other against the buildings on the opposite side of the street, as a line of children walked out of the scribes' shop.

The first two in line were well groomed and held their chins high as they led the other children. The rest did not look so proud to be standing behind the sorcerer. The youngest of them had tears still streaming down her cheeks, and others were puffy-eyed, as though they'd only just been convinced to stop crying.

I held my breath until the last child in line—a boy as old as myself who glared at the sorcerer's back—shut the door behind him. Neither of the boys I'd been captured with stood on the porch.

Keep running. Wherever you are, keep running.

I wished I could somehow speed their journey, but all I could do was send up a silent plea to the stars that they'd stay safe and hidden.

"These children will come with me to Ilara," the sorcerer said. "They will be trained, protected, and provided the best lives the Guilds can offer. They will grow into members of the Sorcerers Guild and will be given the privilege of serving Ilbrea."

A hint of movement toward the back of the crowd caught my eye. A boy with bright blond hair snuck slowly through the frightened horde.

"Cal?" I sank down below the roofline as my heart thundered in my chest.

"The families of these magically gifted children are honored to have their bloodline accepted into the Guilds," the sorcerer said. "A gift many dream of, and few ever achieve."

I peeked back over the ledge.

The blond boy was still slipping slowly through the crowd, craning his neck as he studied the faces of everyone he passed. He looked in my direction.

It was Cal. His face was drawn, and worry creased his brow.

"What are you doing here, Cal?" I whispered.

"There are some who would hide their magic from us," the sorcerer said. "I understand that change, especially for a child, can be frightening. But to those who would keep a gifted child from the sorcerers, I beg you not to give in to that fear. The damage that can be done by unskilled, untrained magic is a risk you do not want to take."

The sorcerer raised her arms high and lightning streaked down from the sky, striking her palms.

"There are people in this town with magic in their blood. I can taste it in the air. Bring them to me. I will wait here until the sun sets." The sorcerer lowered her hands. A chill wind blew down from the north. "When night has fallen, anyone found harboring magic, or those who possess the gift, will be considered complicit in whatever damage and death the untrained will cause."

She turned and walked back into the scribes' shop. The children filed in after her, looking more like prisoners than anyone who had been granted a great honor.

I rolled over and lay with my back pressed to the roof. I dragged my hands over my face as though the movement could somehow replace food and a decent night's sleep in getting my mind to work properly.

I needed to find Emmet. He was the reason I'd come to Nantic.

Cal lurked below, no doubt searching for me.

Did Lily send him, or did he ride all this way on his own?

It didn't really matter either way. There was no chance I was going to have a chat with him on a street lined by soldiers guarding a mad sorcerer.

"Just find Emmet." I rolled onto my stomach and began lowering myself to the lip of the roof. "Find Emmet and move on from there."

The scabs on my fingers cracked as I climbed slowly down the backside of the dress shop, careful to skirt around the windows cutting through the stone.

"By the Guilds, what are you doing?" a woman squawked up at me when I was eight feet off the ground. "You're a thief, you're—"

"I'm not, ma'am." I jumped the rest of the way down. "Honestly, I'm not."

The woman clutched her basket to her chest.

"I was traveling alone and got spooked last night. I was taught to be afraid of men once night falls. I didn't know where else to go to be safe, so I climbed up and hoped no one would find me."

The woman nodded, her winkled cheeks bouncing from the effort. "I suppose no one would find you up there."

"They didn't."

Her gaze moved down to my hands, and she backed away.

I glanced down. Blood seeped from the cuts the knife had left behind, staining my fingers red.

"I'm trying to find my brother." I tucked my hands behind my back. "He works for the blacksmith in town. Can you tell me which way that is?"

The woman pointed west.

"Thank you." I gave her a little curtsy and hurried away before she could scream for the soldiers.

The alley I scurried down ran behind the dress shop and other businesses along the main road. Other, shorter buildings blocked the east side of the path. The whole thing had a scent of rot and human filth that sent bile to my throat.

Still, I lingered in the alley, trying to summon the nerve to cut across the main road.

"Don't be a chivving idiot, Ena." I pressed my back to the clapboard of a shop and peered out into the open.

Most of the crowd had dispersed after the sorcerer finished her display. Those that lingered huddled in groups, whispering among themselves.

The idea that they could be plotting to hand one of their own over to the Guilds sent a wave of fury rolling through my stomach.

Every nerve in my body shook with the urge to run onto the street and shout that anyone who even considered turning a child over to the sorcerer was a traitor to all common folk in Ilbrea. But I'd seen people whipped for saying far less too near soldiers' ears.

I gave one last look for Cal and stepped out onto the road. I kept my hands in my pockets, hiding the blood on my fingers, and locked my gaze forward as though I knew exactly where I was going.

The knife swung in my pocket as I walked. I could feel the blade beginning to slice through the fabric, but I didn't have anywhere else to tuck it and didn't fancy abandoning the one thing I owned besides the clothes on my back.

"No!" The scream carried down the road before I'd reached the far side.

Four people dragged a girl toward the waiting soldiers.

"Let go of me!" the girl yelled. "I said, let go."

A crack like thunder split the air, and the people holding her stumbled back as an invisible something struck me in the center of the chest.

The scraping of the soldiers' swords clearing their sheaths shot fear into my spine as I coughed, trying to regain my breath.

The girl scrambled to her feet, her bright red hair flying behind her as she sprinted away.

"Catch her." One of the people who had held the girl pointed after her. "She's got magic."

The soldiers hadn't needed to be told, they'd already taken off after her.

I wrapped my fingers around the hilt of my knife, desperately trying to think of a way I might be able to help the girl.

But the door to the scribes' shop banged open, and the

sorcerer stepped onto the street, her purple robes billowing around her.

"Stop." The air shook with the force of her command. A ball of brilliant light flew from her hands and soared past the bystanders, through the soldiers, and surrounded the girl.

I could only hear the girl's scream for a moment before the sound was swallowed by the sphere.

Lights danced within the orb as the girl struggled to break free. She kicked back as the sphere lifted from the ground and began to shrink, squeezing in, forcing her to curl into a tight ball.

"That's better." The sorcerer beckoned the sphere toward her. It floated to the sorcerer's side like a bubble blown on a gentle wind. "There is no need to fear, child. The magic in your blood can be frightening. But we'll teach you. We'll take you home."

The girl in the sphere glared at the sorcerer with an expression I knew all too well.

The sorcerer smiled, then blew the orb into the shop, walking in after it and shutting the door behind her.

11

There is a hatred burning deep in my soul. A loathing bred from years of watching the people around me suffer at the hands of the Guilds.

They tax away our lands. Make us pay more than anyone can afford for the simple privileges of getting married, naming our children, and burying our dead. Their soldiers attack us for the slightest offense, then come back through town seizing our young men to swell their ranks. But the common soldiers, they're nothing more than cannon fodder. None of our boys ever come home.

If a girl should get pregnant with no man to marry her, they'll ship her off to the island of Ian Ayres, where she'll give birth in a terrible place. I would hope the legends I've heard of that hell aren't true, but I'm too familiar with the Guilds. I cannot doubt any suffering attributed to their hand. And there is no one to ask for an accurate tale of the bastards' island. None of those girls ever come home, either.

I'd never thought much about the children the sorcerers take. It had always seemed a faraway illusion—a bit of a story where magic existed alongside the suffering in Ilbrea.

But I knew the look on that girl's face, recognized the burning in her heart. She was not privileged. She was not lucky. She was a girl who had been handed to demons and would fight for her freedom with every drop of blood she had.

12

I hesitated, standing there on the road, wanting to do something and knowing there was nothing a girl with a knife could do against a line of soldiers and a sorcerer.

The blade weighed heavy in my pocket. It seemed like such a foolish thing to carry if there wasn't anything I could actually do with it. I slipped between two shops and leaned into the shadows, wishing I could fade into them forever.

Part of me expected to hear Cal calling my name. Part of me wished it would be Lily shouting for me, threatening to flay me alive if I didn't go back to Harane with her at once.

The only thing to find me in the alley was a raven.

He landed on a stack of empty barrels and glared at me with his black eyes.

Caw.

Caw.

Caw.

The creature screamed at me. It was only an animal's call, but I could hear the bird's meaning.

Coward.

Coward.

Coward.

I sat on a barrel beside the bird, spitting on my fingers and using the underside of my skirt to wipe away as much blood as I could.

"What do you propose I do?" I asked the bird.

Caw.

"Very helpful." I nodded. "Glad you took the time to bother me. I've had such a pleasant journey, it does seem time to shake things up a bit. See if I can get myself hanged before I reach Emmet."

There were deep cuts on two of my fingers, but I managed to wipe away enough of the blood that I didn't look like I'd stabbed anyone.

"Do you want to help me then?"

The bird shot off into the sky.

"How lucky you are to be able to flee." I ran my hands over my hair, trying to get myself into a reasonable order before heading for the far side of the alley.

It wasn't backed by a row of buildings as the path behind the dress shop had been, but rather opened up onto another road. Three massive carriages waited behind the scribes' shop, all with purple curtains to cover their windows. Soldiers stood guard around the carriages and back door of the shop.

"What were you expecting, Ena?" I shut my eyes, reasoning through all the different ways I could end up dead.

I'd absolutely no chance of leading a dozen children through the soldiers. They were too well guarded for such a thing. But I couldn't stomach abandoning them with no hope.

"You're a fool, Ena. A chivving fool with a chivving death wish." I squared my shoulders, smiled, and stepped out onto the road behind the scribes' shop.

I am pretty. With a well-made face and gentle curves that men often gape at. Lily liked to remind me beauty is a curse, a useless thing that only causes more pain. But there are advantages to being alluring if you're brave enough to use them.

My skin crawled as the soldiers caught sight of me. I could feel them examining me, studying the scant bit of skin I'd left visible for them.

"Excuse me." I stopped at the youngest, most attractive soldier, giving a little curtsy and a shy grin. "I was hoping to speak to the sorcerer."

"Speak to the sorcerer?"

I wondered if the soldier would have used such a kind tone if I'd been a man.

"I have…" I glanced around the road. "I have a few questions, about how to spot someone who might be hiding magic."

"I'm a guard for the sorcerers," the soldier said. "I'd be happy to help."

"I just…" I bit my bottom lip and wrinkled my brow. "I can't be seen talking in the open like this. I might get in trouble."

This time it was the soldier who looked around the street. "Are you afraid of them?"

"Yes, I mean, I'm not sure if I should be," I said. "If I could just see the sorcerer, then I'd know if I'm right. If I'm not, there's no danger. But if I am, I don't want anyone to get hurt."

The soldier stepped closer to me, lowering his voice. "Tell me who it is, and we'll go see to them. There's no reason for you to be afraid."

"No." I backed away. "No, I can't do that. I'm sure I'm wrong anyway."

I tucked my chin and turned to go, heading back toward the alley I'd come through.

"Stop." Bootfalls pounded after me.

My body tensed as I waited to be grabbed, tossed to the ground, and whipped for keeping information from the Guilds.

"We can talk inside if you'd feel safer." The soldier took my elbow, steering me toward the back door of the scribes' shop.

13

I had never been in a scribes' shop before. I had been too young to handle purchasing the papers for my parents' burials and had never had any other cause in my life to be forced into dealing with a scribe.

The back office smelled of fresh parchment and cheap ink. Sunlight poured into the workroom through the wide windows in the back of the building. Bookcases covered one wall and a rack for scrolls and files another. A set of three desks, one far larger than the other two, sat empty. They'd been left pristine, all the papers perfectly stacked and inkwells closed.

There wasn't even a hint of an ink stain on any of the desks or a single scratch from someone pushing too hard on their pen. I studied the perfection of the desks, trying to keep my gaze from sliding to the floating orb in the corner.

The red-haired girl was still trapped inside, curled up in a ball.

It's no different than what Nirra and Shem did to me.

I swallowed my rage, forcing my face to stay pleasant.

There were three soldiers in the room. The one who had brought me inside and two who stood in front of five of the sorcerer children. The children sat against the wall, each looking somewhere between terrified, furious, and numb.

"You don't need to speak to the sorcerer," the handsome soldier said. "If you suspect someone, you can tell me."

"She's obligated to tell you," one of the other soldiers said. "As a citizen of Ilbrea, it is her duty."

"There's nothing to tell." I backed toward the wall. "I've made a mistake. I should just go."

My heel hit something hard. I leaned back against the bookcase, pressing myself as far away from the soldier as I could.

"Who do you suspect has magic?" the handsome soldier said. "If you're wrong, there's no harm done."

"Easy for you to say. You're a man and a Guilded soldier." I tucked my hands behind my back, careful not to open the wounds on my fingers as I searched for a gap between the book spines. "Please, I'm trying to do the right thing. I just need to speak to the sorcerer."

"It is not your place to demand—"

The door behind the children opened, and the sorcerer stepped into the room.

My breath caught in my chest. Seeing her from the roof was nothing like being trapped inside with her.

It was as though the magic that had caught lightning in her hands still crackled around her. Her scent filled the room like something between the air after a storm and the wind racing through a mountain pass.

"Loud noises agitate the children," the sorcerer said. "I've explained the importance of keeping them calm."

The soldiers tucked their chins, withering under her glare.

"I am sorry, sorcerer." The soldier who had yelled bowed.

"This girl would like to speak to you," the handsome soldier said before the other could continue. "She thinks she may know someone who's hiding magic."

The sorcerer looked to me for the first time.

Her eyes were bright green, a kind of color I'd never seen on a person before. She looked at me for a long moment before speaking. "Who?"

"I have questions first." My words came out stronger than I could have hoped.

"The questions are for me to ask," the sorcerer said.

"Then I'm afraid I cannot answer you." I held my head high and dropped my hands to my sides, abandoning my search of the tightly packed bookcase.

"You don't have a choice." The sorcerer stepped toward me.

"You asked us to come in good faith," I said, "asked us to tell you if we suspected anyone of hiding magic."

"It is your duty," the sorcerer said.

I laughed. "Do you think people will be more or less willing to do their duty if they find out the price of coming forward is being treated poorly by the ones they're trying to help? I have come in good faith to speak to you. Will you allow it or not?"

"You're cheeky." The sorcerer smiled. The curve of her lips sent ice up my spine. "And lucky. I could have you whipped for speaking to me like that."

"You could," I said. "But I wouldn't tell you anything."

"You'd be surprised." The sorcerer gestured for me to sit at the largest of the scribes' desks.

I bundled my pockets into the front of my skirt as I sat. There wasn't a drawer in the front of the desk. It was only a flat table with a surface that could be tipped up to a slant.

"What questions do you want to ask?" The sorcerer stood opposite me, staring down at me as though battling with whether or not to set me on fire.

"How do you know when someone has magic?" I looked to the children along the wall.

The boy near my age who'd been last out the door sat among them. His gaze moved between the sorcerer and me as he regarded us both with similar loathing.

The soldiers guarding the children had turned back to watching their charges. The soldier nearest the boy kicked him in the hip.

The boy winced but didn't make a sound.

"That's the wrong question to ask," the sorcerer said.

"But the children all seem so normal." I stared at the boy, willing him to look back at me. "I thought sorcerers would look different, special somehow."

The boy glared up at me as the sorcerer laughed.

"Magic is in the blood, not displayed upon the skin." The sorcerer paced on her side of the desk. "There is no one physical trait that marks a sorcerer."

I pulled the knife from my pocket, tipping my hand so the boy could see.

His eyes grew wide.

"So the only way to know for certain that a person has magic is to see them use it?" I looked back at the sorcerer.

"Unless you are powerfully magical, as I am, yes." The sorcerer stopped pacing.

I tucked my hand under the lip of the desk, hiding the blade.

"Like calls to like." The sorcerer raised a hand, and the girl in the sphere floated toward her. "The magic within this child resonates out into the world, and my magic is strong enough that I can feel it."

"If you can feel it, why ask us for help at all? Why can't you just ride through town and go into the homes where there's magic?"

"Mind your tone." The sorcerer waved a hand and a stinging struck my cheek.

The knife slipped in my grip. I fumbled for it, slicing my palm on the blade. I winced at the pain, and the sorcerer smiled.

"Magic is not a mating call, you insolent child." The sorcerer planted her hands on the desk and leaned toward me. "It is bigger than being able to pinpoint a person on a map, and more complicated than your weak mind can understand."

I gritted my teeth, biting back the string of curses I longed to scream.

"Can sorcerers toy with a weak mind like mine?" I asked.

The sorcerer tipped her head back and laughed.

I ran my blood-slicked fingers along the inside of the desk, feeling for the hinge to tilt the work top.

"You've been reading fairy stories," the sorcerer said.

"What do you mean?" I asked. "The children all looked so cheerful on the porch. Didn't you work any magic on them to make them smile?"

She raised her hand again. This time the stinging struck the other cheek.

I hunched over, savoring my moment of gasping in pain as I dug the tip of the knife into the side of the hinge, pushing the blade in deep enough to stay without my holding it.

"So, a sorcerer couldn't lure you into doing something foolish?" I sat up. "They couldn't addle your mind?" I pulled my hand back out from under the table, clenching my empty fist and letting it hang by my side.

"It appears your mind is already addled," the sorcerer said. "Stop wasting my time and speak plainly."

A pressure squeezed around my ribs, pressing the air out of my body.

"Stop." My heart raced as panic set in. The sorcerer was going to murder me in the unblemished scribes' shop.

"Speak." The sorcerer smiled.

The pressure around my ribs tightened until it felt like my bones might snap.

"I met a man outside of town," I coughed. "He said he was a sorcerer. I didn't want to believe him."

I gulped in air as the pressure left my lungs.

"Was he a Guilded sorcerer?"

"No." I leaned as far back as my chair would allow. "He wasn't wearing purple robes."

"What did he say to you?" The sorcerer stared into my eyes.

I longed to hide from the fury behind their green.

"He wanted me to come into his tent. Told me that he was a sorcerer, that he was going to meet a pack of other unguilded sorcerers a few miles from here. Said he could show me wonderful magic if I'd go into his tent. I thought he was lying, so I ran away. But…" I looked up to the white painted ceiling. "If a sorcerer can't lure you, then maybe he really does have magic and wasn't just trying to get me to lift my skirt."

"Where did you meet him?" the sorcerer said.

"Please, you can't tell my parents." I forced tears down my cheeks. "If they find out I left town at all, they'll throw me out of the house, and I've nowhere to go."

"Where was he?" The sorcerer raised a hand, and the iron vice of pressure squeezed around my ribs again.

"You have to promise." I fought to speak as I struggled to drag in air.

"Your whoring is a problem for Ian Ayres, not for me," the sorcerer sneered. "Tell me where he was and get out of my sight."

"Two hours walk south." I collapsed against the table as the pressure around my lungs disappeared. "He had a tent set up on the west side of the road. He had no horse or wagon I could see. I don't know how he was traveling."

"Get out," the sorcerer spat.

"Thank you, ma'am." I stumbled up from my seat. "Best of luck on your journey." I glanced toward the boy on the floor. "I hope what I've given you can be of use."

I ran for the door, tossed it open, and kept running until the scent of the sorcerer left me.

I didn't stay close enough to the scribes' shop to see if the soldiers rode out to search for the unguilded sorcerer I'd warned them of. The sounds of men shouting and horses stomping came from that direction, but I'd passed beyond the ability to watch and didn't fancy doubling back to see if my lie had taken hold.

I leaned against the wide-cut log front of a woodworker's shop and considered trying to climb to the roof to see if I could get a view of the soldiers, but blood had started dripping from my still-clenched hand. The longer I stood in the shade of the shop, the worse the stinging on my palm became.

Water, strong liquor, bandages. All things I needed—none of which I had.

Gritting my teeth, I unclenched my hand. The wound wasn't awful, but it bled too much to be ignored and needed a good cleaning.

"Emmet's going to murder me." I laughed.

The touch of joy at imagining showing up to Emmet's, dripping blood from my hand, laid a little veil over the fear the last two days had brought.

I remembered everything that had happened. I don't think

anything could ever wipe the memory of the terror I'd felt completely away. But a bubble of hope dared to bloom in my chest, blurring the images I wished I could forget.

Hissing through my teeth at the sting, I clenched my fist to hide the worst of the blood and walked farther west.

There was a shop with cakes displayed in the window and a tavern with a barrel hanging over the door. A little girl ran past. A dog scampered at her heels, his tongue hanging from his mouth. The child seemed happy, the tavern well trafficked, and the cake shop had so many sweets on display, they could have made the entire village of Harane ill.

This will be my home. And I will learn every inch of its beauties.

The sharp clang of metal on metal reached my ears before I could actually see the blacksmith's shop.

I doubled my pace as the clang struck again.

"Ena!"

The familiar voice froze me in place.

"Ena."

I didn't turn to look as Cal's footsteps pounded toward me.

"Ena, are you all right?" Cal took my face in his hands before I could speak. "I've been terrified. I came up the mountain road, and I didn't see you. I've been searching all over town for you."

"I don't know why. I didn't ask you to come." I moved his hands away from my face.

"Did you think I'd just let you dis—" He caught hold of my bloody hand. "You're hurt. What's happened to you?"

"Nothing." I clutched my hand to my chest. "I fell and cut it, that's all."

"You need to clean it."

"You think I don't know that?" I stepped around Cal.

"Where are you going?"

"To Emmet." I strode toward the clanging. "He works for a blacksmith. They'll have something I can use as a bandage."

"Ena, no." Cal took my shoulder, stopping me mid-step. "I've got a room at a tavern. We can go there, get your hand washed and bandaged up."

"No." I shook free of him.

"Then we'll go where you stayed last night." Cal darted around to stand in front of me.

"I don't think that would work." I moved to step around Cal, but he dodged into my path.

"Then come with me. The owner of the tavern where I stayed baked fresh biscuits this morning. We'll have a proper meal. We can talk—"

"No, Cal." I tried again to step around him, and again he blocked my path. "I'm sorry, all right? I'm sorry I left without telling you. And I'm sorry that hurt you. But I am going to see my brother, so get out of my way or I'll smear my bloody palm on you."

"Ena…"

I dodged around him and headed toward the clanging.

A sign came into view. The words *Ender's Smith* had been worked into beautiful, black, swirling metal. Emmet had never told me the sign for the shop was so fancy.

I quickened my step, holding back my urge to shout Emmet's name.

"Ena, please don't." Cal chased after me.

"Go home, Cal."

The heat struck me as I stopped outside the open doors. The scent of burning coal, with a sweet something I couldn't name hovering beneath, filled my lungs as I stepped into the shop.

Two men flanked an anvil, hammers in their grips. A boy worked the bellows, and another man stood at a table in the back. Emmet was nowhere in sight.

The man at the table looked up. "Can I help you?"

"Yes." I stepped farther into the shop, searching the shadows for Emmet. "I'm here to see—"

"Oh." The man looked over my shoulder. His brow furrowed.

"What?" I glanced behind to find Cal lingering just outside the entrance. "I'm looking for my brother, Emmet Ryeland."

"He's not here." The man walked out from behind the table.

"That's fine," I said. "I can wait."

"No, you can't," the man said.

"I'll wait outside then. Do you know when he'll be back?"

The man looked over my shoulder to Cal again.

"I won't stay here bothering you." I stepped in front of the man to stop him from looking at chivving Cal. "Just tell me when he'll be back, and you won't have to—"

"He's not coming back," Cal said.

"Cal, this has got nothing to do with you." I rounded on him.

"Boy's right," the man said. "I haven't seen Emmet Ryeland in more than a year."

"Of course you have." I turned back to the man. "Just tell me where my brother is, and I'll leave."

"The gods only know where Emmet's gone," the man said. "He left without a note or goodbye. Woke up one morning to find the money he owed on my table, and that was it."

"No." I pointed to the man. "Do not lie to me."

"What happened to your hand, girl?" The man reached for me.

"Don't touch me!"

"Ena—" Cal laid a hand on my shoulder.

"I said don't touch me." I jerked away from him. "Did you pay him to lie, Cal? Are you that desperate for me to go back to Harane?"

Cal flinched like I'd used the sorcerer's magic to strike him. "I came to this shop last night looking for you. I found out Emmet was gone then."

"No, he's not," I said. "He came to visit me last month. I saw him. You saw him. He stayed later in the day than he usually dares. I was worried about him being on the road, but he said it didn't matter, he could find his way to Nantic in the dark. It's only the one road. That's what he said. He said he was coming back here."

"He lied." Cal reached for me.

"Emmet wouldn't do that."

"He did," the man said. "Don't know why. All I know is he's not here."

"You're a liar!" I shouted.

"He's not," Cal said. "Ena, I'm sorry. I'm so sorry, but your brother isn't here."

There was something in the sadness in Cal's eyes, a pain that went beyond his hurt at my leaving. Cal was too good, too kind—that sort of wound he could only suffer at the pain of another.

"Then where is he?" The scent of the shop had gotten too heavy.

The men began striking their hammers again. The clanging pounded through my head.

"Cal, where is he?"

"I don't know." Cal reached for me again.

I didn't back away.

"He must have told someone." I looked to the blacksmith. "There's got to be someone in Nantic he told where he was going."

The smith shook his head. "Far as anyone here knows, he's sailed across the Arion Sea. I'm sorry, girl."

The man turned and went back to his table, like he had work to be done that was somehow more important than finding my brother.

Cal guided me out of the shop, his hand laid gently on my back as though afraid I might crack.

The bright sunlight on the street seemed absurd. There should not be sunlight and birds cawing when someone has disappeared from the world.

"We'll go to the tavern," Cal said. "We'll get your hand cleaned and some food for you to eat."

"No." I shook free of him. "I can't go to a tavern. I have to find Emmet." A pain struck me deep in my chest. "I don't know how to find him. Ilbrea is massive. He could have gone to sea. How am I supposed to find him?"

"I don't think you can." Cal pressed his lips to my forehead. He wrapped his arms around me and let me lean into his warmth. "I'm sorry, Ena."

We stood like that for a long time.

I searched every face we passed on the way to the tavern. I asked the woman behind the bar if she knew where Emmet Ryeland had gone. She gave me a sad smile and a cup of strong liquor.

I was too numb to fight when Cal brought me to the horse I was to ride back to Harane. He'd brought two. One for him and one for me. Like he'd known I would be too tired to walk all the way home.

The purple-curtained carriages were still behind the scribes' shop when the horse carried me past. Most of the soldiers were missing.

We rode by them on the way south. They'd torn through Shem's tent, leaving scraps on the ground. There wasn't enough caring left in me to laugh at the soldiers standing at the edge of the woods, too afraid to tempt the ghosts that lurked within the mountains.

There wasn't enough left of me to do anything but survive.

There were no candles burning in the windows to greet us as we rode back into Harane. I didn't want there to be.

I was returning to a place where there was nothing for me but death. I would watch the people around me die until the Guilds put a rope around my neck.

Cal kissed me as he led me to Lily's garden gate, careful not to squeeze my bandaged hand. He whispered promises of happy days, of light and joy he would help me find. I made myself smile for him as I shut the gate behind me.

I sat alone in the garden until the sun came up, trying to find a way to resign myself to the fate the stars had given me.

If there was nothing for me but death, then I would face it bravely. I would not cower as I waited for the end. I would stride defiantly through my life and glare into the eyes of the beasts who came to slaughter me.

But the fate I imagined as I sat in the darkness was not to be mine. If the sky itself had opened and told me the miles I would travel, the magic I would see, and the battles I would fight, I would have laughed at the gods.

The gods would have laughed right back.

The ways of magic are unknowable. The mountains themselves are alive with power. And soon, very soon, I would meet
the man who would be my undoing, and find the love that would
remake my soul.

Ena's journey continues in Ember and Stone. *Read on for a sneak
preview.*

ENA NEVER HOPED FOR A PEACEFUL LIFE.

SHE NEVER DREAMT SHE'D BECOME A
KILLER EITHER.

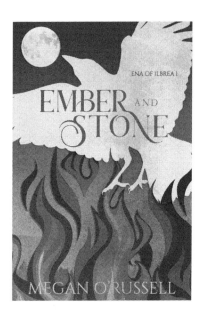

Continue reading for a sneak peek of *Ember and Stone*.

The crack of the whip sent the birds scattering into the sky. They cawed their displeasure at the violence of the men below as they flew over the village and to the mountains beyond.

The whip cracked again.

Aaron did well. He didn't start to moan until the fourth lash. By the seventh, he screamed in earnest.

No one had given him a belt to bite down on. There hadn't been time when the soldiers hauled him from his house and tied him to the post in the square.

I clutched the little wooden box of salve hidden in my pocket, letting the corners bite deep into my palm.

The soldier passed forty lashes, not caring that Aaron's back had already turned to pulp.

I squeezed my way to the back of the crowd, unwilling to watch Aaron's blood stain the packed dirt.

Behind the rest of the villagers, children cowered in their mother's skirts, hiding from the horrors the Guilds' soldiers brought with them.

I didn't know how many strokes Aaron had been sentenced

to. I didn't want to know. I made myself stop counting how many times the whip sliced his back.

Bida, Aaron's wife, wept on the edge of the crowd. When his screams stopped, hers grew louder.

The women around Bida held her back, keeping her out of reach of the soldiers.

My stomach stung with the urge to offer comfort as she watched her husband being beaten by the men in black uniforms. But, with the salve tucked in my pocket, hiding in the back was safest.

I couldn't give Bida the box unless Aaron survived. Spring hadn't fully arrived, and the plants Lily needed to make more salves still hadn't bloomed. The tiny portion of the stuff hidden in my pocket was worth more than someone's life, especially if that person wasn't going to survive even with Lily's help.

Lily's orders had been clear—wait and see if Aaron made it through. Give Bida the salve if he did. If he didn't, come back home and hide the wooden box under the floorboards for the next poor soul who might need it.

Aaron fell to the ground. Blood leaked from a gash under his arm.

The soldier raised his whip again.

I sank farther into the shadows, trying to comfort myself with the beautiful lie that I could never be tied to the post in the village square, though I knew the salve clutched in my hand would see me whipped at the post as quickly as whatever offense the soldiers had decided Aaron had committed.

When my fingers had gone numb from gripping the box, the soldier stopped brandishing his whip and turned to face the crowd.

"We did not come here to torment you," the soldier said. "We came here to protect Ilbrea. We came here to protect the Guilds. We are here to provide peace to all the people of this great country.

This man committed a crime, and he has been punished. Do not think me cruel for upholding the law." He wrapped the bloody whip around his hand and led the other nine soldiers out of the square.

Ten soldiers. It had only taken ten of them to walk into our village and drag Aaron from his home. Ten men to tie him to the post and leave us all helpless as they beat a man who'd lived among us all his life.

The soldiers disappeared, and the crowd shifted in toward Aaron. I couldn't hear him crying or moaning over the angry mutters of the crowd.

His wife knelt by his side, wailing.

I wound my way forward, ignoring the stench of fear that surrounded the villagers.

Aaron lay on the ground, his hands still tied around the post. His back had been flayed open by the whip. His flesh looked more like something for a butcher to deal with than an illegal healer like me.

I knelt by his side, pressing my fingers to his neck to feel for a pulse.

Nothing.

I wiped my fingers on the cleanest part of Aaron's shirt I could find and weaved my way back out of the crowd, still clutching the box of salve in my hand.

Carrion birds gathered on the rooftops near the square, scenting the fresh blood in the air. They didn't know Aaron wouldn't be food for them. The villagers of Harane had yet to fall so low as to leave our own out as a feast for the birds.

There was no joy in the spring sun as I walked toward Lily's house on the eastern edge of the village.

I passed by the tavern, which had already filled with men who didn't mind we hadn't reached midday. I didn't blame them for hiding in there. If they could find somewhere away from the torment of the soldiers, better on them for seizing it. I only hoped there weren't any soldiers laughing inside the tavern's walls.

I followed the familiar path home. Along our one, wide dirt road, past the few shops Harane had to offer, to the edge of the village where only fields and pastures stood between us and the forest that reached up the eastern mountains' slopes.

It didn't take long to reach the worn wooden house with the one giant tree towering out front. It didn't take long to reach anywhere in the tiny village of Harane.

Part of me hated knowing every person who lived nearby. Part of me wished the village were smaller. Then maybe we'd fall off the Guilds' maps entirely.

As it was, the Guilds only came when they wanted to collect our taxes, to steal our men to fight their wars, or to find some other sick pleasure in inflicting agony on people who wanted nothing more than to survive. Or if their business brought them far enough south on the mountain road they had to pass through our home on their way to torment someone else.

I allowed myself a moment to breathe before facing Lily. I blinked away the images of Aaron covered in blood and shoved them into a dark corner with the rest of the wretched things it was better not to ponder.

Lily barely glanced up as I swung open the gate and stepped into the back garden. Dirt covered her hands and skirt. Her shoulders were hunched from the hours spent planting our summer garden. She never allowed me to help with the task. Everything had to be carefully planned, keeping the vegetables toward the outermost edges. Hiding the plants she could be hanged for in the center, where soldiers were less likely to spot the things she grew to protect the people of our village. The people the soldiers were so eager to hurt.

"Did he make it?" Lily stretched her shoulders back and brushed the dirt off her weathered hands.

I held the wooden box out as my response. Blood stained the

corners. It wasn't Aaron's blood. It was mine. Cuts marked my hand where I'd squeezed the box too tightly.

Lily glared at my palm. "You'd better go in and wrap your hand. If you let it get infected, I'll have to treat you with the salve, and you know we're running out."

I tucked the box back into my pocket and went inside, not bothering to argue that I could heal from a tiny cut. I didn't want to look into Lily's wrinkled face and see the glimmer of pity in her eyes.

The inside of the house smelled of herbs and dried flowers. Their familiar scent did nothing to drive the stench of blood and fear from my nose.

A pot hung over the stove, waiting with whatever Lily had made for breakfast.

My stomach churned at the thought of eating. I needed to get out. Out of the village, away from the soldiers.

I pulled up the loose floorboard by the stove and tucked the salve in between the other boxes, tins, and vials. I grabbed my bag off the long, wooden table and shoved a piece of bread and a waterskin into it for later. I didn't bother grabbing a coat or shawl. I didn't care about getting cold.

I have to get out.

I was back through the door and in the garden a minute later. Lily didn't even look up from her work. "If you're running into the forest, you had better come back with something good."

"I will," I said. "I'll bring you back all sorts of wonderful things. Just make sure you save some dinner for me."

I didn't need to ask her to save me food. In all the years I'd lived with her, Lily had never let me go hungry. But she was afraid I would run away into the forest and never return. Or maybe it was me that feared I might disappear into the trees and never come back. Either way, I felt myself relax as I stepped out of the garden and turned my feet toward the forest.

The mountains rose up beyond the edge of the trees, fierce towers I could never hope to climb. No one else from the village would ever even dream of trying such a thing.

The soldiers wouldn't enter the woods. The villagers rarely dared to go near them. The forest was where darkness and solitude lay. A quiet place where the violence of the village couldn't follow me.

I skirted farmers' fields and picked my way through the pastures. No one bothered me as I climbed over the fences they built to keep in their scarce amounts of sheep and cows.

No one kept much livestock. They couldn't afford it in the first place. And besides, if the soldiers saw that one farmer had too many animals, they would take the beasts as taxes. Safer to be poor. Better for your belly to go empty than for the soldiers to think you had something to give.

I moved faster as I got past the last of the farmhouses and beyond the reach of the stench of animal dung.

When I was a very little girl, my brother had told me that the woods were ruled by ghosts. That none of the villagers dared to cut down the trees or venture into their shelter for fear of being taken by the dead and given a worse fate than even the Guilds could provide.

I'd never been afraid of ghosts, and I'd wandered through the woods often enough to be certain that no spirits roamed the eastern mountains.

When I first started going into the forest, I convinced myself I was braver than everyone else in Harane. I was an adventurer, and they were cowards.

Maybe I just knew better. Maybe I knew that no matter what ghosts did, they could never match the horrors men inflict on each other. What I'd seen them do to each other.

By the time I was a hundred feet into the trees, I could no longer see the village behind me. I couldn't smell anything but the fresh scent of damp earth as the little plants fought for survival in the fertile spring ground. I knew my way through the woods well enough I didn't need to bother worrying about which direction to go. It was more a question of which direction I wanted to chase the gentle wind.

I could go and find fungi for Lily to make into something useful, or I could climb. If I went quickly, I would have time to climb and still be able to find something worth Lily getting herself hanged for.

Smiling to myself, I headed due east toward the steepest part of the mountains near our village. Dirt soon covered the hem of my skirt, and mud squelched beneath my shoes, creeping in through the cracked leather of the soles. I didn't mind so much. What the cold could do to me was nothing more than a refreshing chance to prove I was still alive. Life existed outside the village, and there was beauty beyond our battered walls.

Bits of green peeked through the brown of the trees as new buds forced their way out of the branches.

I stopped, staring up at the sky, marveling at the beauty hidden within our woods.

Birds chirped overhead. Not the angry cawing of birds of

death, but the beautiful songs of lovebirds who had nothing more to worry about than tipping their wings up toward the sky.

A gray and blue bird burst from a tree, carrying his song deeper into the forest.

A stream gurgled to one side of me. The snap of breaking branches came from the other. I didn't change my pace as the crackling came closer.

I headed south to a steeper slope where I had to use my hands to pull myself up the rocks.

I moved faster, outpacing the one who lumbered through the trees behind me. A rock face cut through the forest, blocking my path. I dug my fingers into the cracks in the stone, pulling myself up. Careful to keep my legs from being tangled in my skirt, I found purchase on the rock with the soft toes of my boots. In a few quick movements, I pushed myself up over the top of the ledge. I leapt to my feet and ran to the nearest tree, climbing up to the highest thick branch.

I sat silently on my perch, waiting to see what sounds would come from below.

A rustle came from the base of the rock, followed by a long string of inventive curses.

I bit my lips together, not allowing myself to call out.

The cursing came again.

"Of all the slitching, vile—" the voice from below growled.

I leaned back against the tree, closing my eyes, reveling in my last few moments of solitude. Those hints of freedom were what I loved most about being able to climb. Going up a tree, out of reach of the things that would catch me.

"Ena," the voice called. "Ena."

I didn't answer.

"Ena, are you going to leave me down here?"

My lips curved into a smile as I bit back my laughter. "I didn't ask you to follow me. You can just go back the way you came."

"I don't want to go back," he said. "Let me come up. At least show me how you did it."

"If you want to chase me, you'd better learn to climb."

I let him struggle for a few more minutes until he threatened to find a pick and crack through the rock wall. I glanced down to find him three feet off the ground, his face bright red as he tried to climb.

"Jump down," I said, not wanting him to fall and break something. I could have hauled him back to the village, but I didn't fancy the effort.

"Help me get up," he said.

"Go south a bit. You'll find an easier path."

I listened to the sounds of him stomping off through the trees, enjoying the bark against my skin as I waited for him to find the way up.

It only took him a few minutes to loop back around to stand under my perch.

Looking at Cal stole my will to flee. His blond hair glistened in the sun. He shaded his bright blue eyes as he gazed up at me.

"Are you happy now?" he said. "I'm covered in dirt."

"If you wanted to be clean, you shouldn't have come into the woods. I never ask you to follow me."

"It would have been wrong of me not to. You shouldn't be coming out here by yourself."

I didn't let it bother me that he thought it was too dangerous for me to be alone in the woods. It was nice to have someone worry about me. Even if he was worried about ghosts that didn't exist.

"What do you think you'd be able to do to help me anyway?" I said.

He stared up at me, hurt twisting his perfect brow.

Cal looked like a god, or something made at the will of the Guilds themselves. His chiseled jaw held an allure to it, the rough stubble on his cheeks luring my fingers to touch its texture.

I twisted around on my seat and dropped down to the ground, reveling in his gasp as I fell.

"You really need to get more used to the woods," I said. "It's a good place to hide."

"What would I have to hide from?" Cal's eyes twinkled, offering a hint of teasing that drew me toward him.

I touched the stubble on his chin, tracing the line of his jaw.

"There are plenty of things to hide from, fool." I turned to tramp farther into the woods.

"Ena," he called after me, "you shouldn't be going so far from home."

"Then don't follow me. Go back." I knew he would follow.

I had known when I passed by his window in the tavern on my way through the village. He always wanted to be near me. That was the beauty of Cal.

I veered closer to the stream.

Cal kept up, though he despised getting his boots muddy.

I always chose the more difficult path to make sure he knew I could outpace him. It was part of our game on those trips into the forest.

I leapt across the stream to a patch of fresh moss just beginning to take advantage of spring.

"Ena." Cal jumped the water and sank down onto the moss I had sought.

I shoved him off of the green and into the dirt.

He growled.

I didn't bother trying to hide my smile. I pulled out tufts of the green moss, tucking them into my bag for Lily.

"If you don't want me to follow you," Cal said, "you can tell me not to whenever you like."

"The forest doesn't belong to me, Cal. You can go where you choose."

He grabbed both my hands and tugged me toward him. I tipped onto him and he shifted, letting me fall onto my back. I caught a glimpse of the sun peering down through the new buds of emerald leaves, and then he was kissing me.

His taste of honey and something a bit deeper filled me. And I forgot about whips and Lily and men bleeding and soldiers coming to kill us.

There was nothing but Cal and me. And the day became beautiful.

Order your copy of Ember and Stone *to continue Ena's journey.*

ESCAPE INTO ADVENTURE

Thank you for reading *Wrath and Wing*. If you enjoyed the book, please consider leaving a review to help other readers find Ena's story.

As always, thanks for reading,

Megan O'Russell

Never miss a moment of the magic and romance.

Join the Megan O'Russell mailing list to stay up to date on all the action by visiting https://www.meganorussell.com/book-signup.

ABOUT THE AUTHOR

 Megan O'Russell is the author of several Young Adult series that invite readers to escape into worlds of adventure. From *Girl of Glass*, which blends dystopian darkness with the heart-pounding danger of vampires, to *Ena of Ilbrea*, which draws readers into an epic world of magic and assassins.

With the *Girl of Glass* series, *The Tethering* series, *The Chronicles of Maggie Trent*, *The Tale of Bryant Adams*, the *Ena of Ilbrea* series, and several more projects planned for 2020, there are always exciting new books on the horizon. To be the first to hear about new releases, free short stories, and giveaways, sign up for Megan's newsletter by visiting the following:

https://www.meganorussell.com/book-signup.

Originally from Upstate New York, Megan is a professional musical theatre performer whose work has taken her across North America. Her chronic wanderlust has led her from Alaska to Thailand and many places in between. Wanting to travel has fostered Megan's love of books that allow her to visit countless new worlds from her favorite reading nook. Megan is also a lyricist and playwright. Information on her theatrical works can be found at RussellCompositions.com.

She would be thrilled to chat with you on Facebook or

Twitter @MeganORussell, elated if you'd visit her website MeganORussell.com, and over the moon if you'd like the pictures of her adventures on Instagram @ORussellMegan.

ALSO BY MEGAN O'RUSSELL

Ice and Sky

Feather and Flame

<u>Guilds of Ilbrea</u>

Inker and Crown

Printed in Great Britain
by Amazon